PARADE

Also by Shuichi Yoshida

Villain

PARADE

SHUICHI YOSHIDA

TRANSLATED
FROM THE JAPANESE
BY PHILIP GABRIEL

Harvill Secker
LONDON

Published by Harvill Secker 2014

2 4 6 8 10 9 7 5 3 1

First published as *Paredo* in Japan by Gentosha Inc., Tokyo, in 2002

First published in Great Britain in 2014 by
HARVILL SECKER
Random House
20 Vauxhall Bridge Road
London SW1V 2SA

www.vintage-books.co.uk

Addresses for companies within The Random House Group Limited can be found at:
www.randomhouse.co.uk/offices.htm

The Random House Group Limited Reg. No. 954009

A CIP catalogue record for this book is available from the British Library

ISBN 9781846552373

The Random House Group Limited supports the Forest Stewardship Council®
(FSC®), the leading international forest-certification organisation. Our books carrying
the FSC label are printed on FSC®-certified paper. FSC is the only forest-certification
scheme supported by the leading environmental organisations, including Greenpeace.
Our paper procurement policy can be found at www.randomhouse.co.uk/environment

Typeset in Electra Lt Std by Palimpsest Book Production Limited,
Falkirk, Stirlingshire

Printed and bound in Great Britain by Clays Ltd, St Ives plc

CAST OF CHARACTERS

RYOSUKE SUGIMOTO (21)
Junior in the economics department of H University.
Presently working part-time at a Mexican restaurant in Shimokitazawa.

KOTOMI OKOCHI (23)
Unemployed.
In love with the popular young actor Tomohiko Maruyama.

MIRAI SOMA (24)
Illustrator and manager of an imported goods store.
Thinking over life from the bottom of a bottle.

SATORU KOKUBO (18)
Works at 'night jobs'.
Selling off his excess youth.

NAOKI IHARA (28)
Employee at an independent film distributor.
Trying to guess who will win the 54th Cannes Film Festival's Palme d'Or.

RYOSUKE SUGIMOTO (21)

1.1

It was such a weird sight. I was on the fourth-floor balcony looking directly down on Kyukoshu Kaido Boulevard, and though thousands of cars passed by here every day, I'd never seen an accident. There's an intersection directly below the balcony, and when the traffic light turned red a car stopped right at the line. The car behind it came to a halt, leaving just the right amount of distance so they didn't collide, and the car behind that one also stopped, leaving the same exact gap. When the light turned green the lead car slowly pulled away, with the second and third cars following at a safe distance, just like they were being pulled along.

I mean, I do the same thing when I'm driving. I step on the brake when the car in front comes to a stop, and don't step on the gas until he starts moving again, no matter how long the light might be green. You can dismiss it as common sense, and accidents don't occur that easily, but still, looking down on the street from above like that, the ordinary movement of cars looked totally weird.

Why, on a beautiful Sunday afternoon, was I staring down at traffic?

That's easy. I was bored.

When I'm bored like this it feels like time isn't going in a straight line but is connected at both ends like a circle, and the time I experienced a while back I'm going through all over again. Maybe this is what people mean when they say that something doesn't have a sense of *reality*. Like, say I leap from this balcony right now. This is the fourth floor, so if I'm lucky I'd get away with a broken bone. If not, I'd be killed instantly. But if time is circular, then even if I'm killed instantly the first time, there's always a second time. Having experienced instant death the first time, maybe the second time I can leap down in a way so I wind up with just a minor sprain. By the third time, though, I'd be tired of it all, and wouldn't even go to the trouble of straddling the railing. But if I don't leap off the balcony, nothing will change. The same old boring time awaits.

It's isn't like there's nothing I want to do on a beautiful Sunday. But if somebody asked what exactly it is I'd like to do, I'd be stuck. Maybe going somewhere I've never been, meeting someone I've never seen before, and talking with them, being so open and honest it's almost embarrassing. It doesn't have to be some cute girl – it could be like Sensei and K in Soseki's novel *Kokoro*, where they struggle and suffer over life and love. Of course I wouldn't want the other person to commit suicide, like Sensei. Give me a carefree optimist any day.

I felt like a slug pasted to the railing, but I managed to peel myself away and head back to my room. I trampled across the unmade futon on the tatami and made my way out to the living room.

Koto, or her back at least, was there, staring intently at a repeat of *A Nurse's Work* on TV. She had on her typical tracksuit that doubled as pyjamas, and she was trimming her split ends. She must have sensed I was there when I came out of my room because she laughed, like she was making fun of me. 'When school's out,' she said, 'college students have nothing to do.' I had a sudden urge to pull the full-length mirror over to her. Let her break out in a clammy sweat when she saw what she looked like.

'I'm going to the store,' I said. 'Anything you want me to pick up?'

I checked my wallet first. With a fistful of split ends in her hand, Koto turned around. 'Store? Why?'

'I don't know,' I answered. 'Just going to flip through some magazines.'

You've got too much time on your hands, I was sure she was going to say, but instead she said, 'Magazines? I think I'll join you.'

'You don't need to.'

'How come?'

'If you tag along, I won't be able to check out the magazines I really want to look at.'

'What exactly are you planning to read?'

Just then the TV screen got all fuzzy. The actress Arisa Mizuki, adorable in a tiny miniskirted nurse's uniform, was racing down a hallway holding an IV, but it looked like she was about to be engulfed in a sandstorm. Our TV isn't working too well these days. It's like the TV is trying to send us a message: *Time to buy a new one, guys*.

'It's *zapping* again,' Koto said, as we watched the screen.

'That isn't what zapping means. Zapping means changing the channels all the time with the remote control. I used that word the other day at college and nobody knew what I was talking about.'

'Then what should we call it?'

'Don't know. It's just that we're the only ones who seem to use it that way.'

Koto leapt to her feet, went over to the TV and gave it a solid smack. The screen wavered, like it was actually in pain, and with her third punch, a smart right hook, it went back to normal.

'You're really good,' I said.

'Huh?'

'You really know how to fix it.'

'The TV? There's a trick to it.'

Koto sat back down on the floor and resumed trimming her split ends.

'Ryosuke, what are your three favourite TV shows? Dramas, I mean,' she said.

'You already asked me that the other day,' I replied, staring at Arisa Mizuki who, on the screen, was still racing down the hallway.

'The last time I asked for your top Monday nine o'clock dramas. Okay, now I'm asking about only the ten o'clock Friday dramas on TBS. For me, it would be *As Long as I Love You*, and *Tell Me You Love Me*. But for the third one, I can't decide between *High School Teachers* and *No Longer Human* . . .'

Arisa Mizuki had changed out of her nurse's uniform so I headed out of the door. Behind me Koto called out, 'You gotta tell me!' She seemed like she was still going to press me for an answer when I got back from the shop so I asked, 'Was *Mismatched Apples* on Fridays at ten?'

'Yeah, it was,' she said.

'Well, then my choice would be *Mismatched Apples*, parts one, two and three,' I said, and left. As soon as I did, I thought I should have asked her what the trick was to fixing the TV. For a second I was about to turn around, but then I changed my mind. It was probably better the TV didn't work, I thought.

Koto was mistaken: college wasn't on spring break, but in the middle of exams. To keep her skin beautiful and to make sure she got enough sleep, Koto always went to bed around the time the eleven o'clock news starts, so she had no idea that, for the last couple of weeks, I'd been staying up late, at the table in the living room, turning a *Line Graph Illustrating Fluctuations in Exchange Rates after the Plaza Accord* into drawings of dragons, and making my Japanese–French dictionary into an animated flip book.

For what it's worth, I commute to college by car. It sounds cool, but no girl would ever be happy to see me sidle up in my car to pick her up for a date. It's a tiny, used Nissan March that I picked up for ¥70,000 when I started college. As soon as I got it I bought a book on lucky names and dubbed her Momoko. Momoko Sugimoto. It takes twenty-five strokes in four characters to write the name, a lucky number. *A very straightforward person, self-reliant*, the handbook said. *Someone who's likeable, filial, and polite to elders. Though there are some health problems related to bronchitis* . . . And sure enough these symptoms showed up the third day after I bought her. After I drive about ten kilometres, Momoko's engine invariably sputters to a stop.

When I'm driving from Chitose Karasuyama to my college in Ichigaya, the ten-kilometre mark is exactly in front of Shinjuku Station. Once my engine died right at the crossing in front of the

Alta building in broad daylight. No matter how much I turned the key, good old Momoko wouldn't budge. The light soon turned green and the guy behind me blared his horn hysterically. I had no choice but to get out and, steering with one hand, huff and puff as I pushed the car. Just because it only cost ¥70,000 doesn't mean it's a light car. People waiting to cross had a good laugh watching me desperately pushing it towards a tour bus stop. But the world's not all bad. As I continued on, my face getting red, the car suddenly seemed lighter and when I turned around there were two older guys, the type I normally wouldn't want to get involved with, pushing Momoko's rear end.

'Get in and use the brake,' one of the guys yelled. 'You're gonna hit something!' I leapt into the driver's seat. We barely avoided slamming into some railings and doing a number on Momoko's face. I leaned out to thank the two men, but they'd already crossed the street and were clambering over the railings in front of Alta. 'Thank you!' I yelled to them, but my shout was drowned out by the noise in front of Shinjuku Station. They didn't turn around, and hurried off in the direction of Kabukicho, the red-light district. They looked like two guys from Saitama City, or maybe Nagareyama City in Chiba. Whenever someone's having car trouble it always seems like it's these kind of tough-guy wannabes who show up out of nowhere and lend a hand.

Which is all a roundabout way of explaining that now, when I drive Momoko, I stop and turn off the engine every nine kilometres. Naturally I haven't taken her on long drives. Now that I own a car, the scope of my activities has actually shrunk.

There aren't any parking spaces at the university, so I have to park along the Imperial Palace moat. It's illegal, of course, and worst-case scenario, you get towed. But not my Momoko. There's a coffee shop next to the moat called Le Fran, and whenever the traffic cops come, the owner of Le Fran reparks Momoko over at the coffee shop car park until they're gone. The reason he's so nice to Momoko, my lovely vehicle who lets delinquents grope her backside, is because he's the one who pawned her off on me, like she was his precious little princess.

Three days ago, when I had a test on trade theory, Le Fran's owner came to Momoko's rescue again. And it was right after the exam that a classmate of mine, Sakuma, who I hadn't seen in a long time, said something again about wanting to see Koto.

Sakuma and I first met during the college entrance ceremony at Budokan, when we happened to sit next to each other, and he's basically my only real friend in college. Sakuma's the one who taught me everything I know about how to live in Tokyo. Like how to ride the trains (there aren't any trains in the town I come from), what to wear (I've already mastered T-shirts and sweatshirts), where the fashionable bars are, how to find lucrative part-time jobs. All those things I learned from him. Not that he led me by the hand, carefully teaching me each point. Take trains, for instance. One when I'd just started college, Sakuma and I took the Yamanote Line after classes. There was something that'd been bothering me ever since I came to Tokyo.

'Where's everybody going?' I asked Sakuma. We were clutching on to the straps in the train as it rolled along. I was referring to all the passengers who were making their way to another car. Now I know that they were all moving to the car that's closest to the exit in the station they were getting out at, but back then I couldn't imagine such a rational way of thinking.

'Who're you talking about?'

Sakuma didn't get why I was confused. I'd been thinking there must be toilets in some other car on the train, and asked him if that was it. It finally dawned on him what I meant.

'Ah, *those* people,' he said nodding. 'They're not going to the loos. They're heading to the snack bar.'

Back then, if Sakuma had told me there was a dining car, even I would have had my doubts, but I could still buy the notion of the Yamanote Line having a snack bar on the train, where they sold canned drinks and newspapers and so on. Chagrined by my naivety, I still haven't told Sakuma how I walked through the Yamanote Line cars day after day in search of this mystery snack bar.

After the exam on trade theory three days ago, Sakuma and I left campus, heading for a pool hall, and stopped by the Lotteria fast food store at Iidabashi.

'Everybody at your place doing okay?' he asked me, his mouth stuffed with a cheeseburger. I don't know how many times I told him not to, but he insisted on sitting cross-legged in restaurants.

'Who do you mean, *everybody*?' I said, deliberately dense.

'Everybody means everybody,' Sakuma pouted.

'Anybody in particular you're asking about?'

I realised I was acting kind of like an arse. 'Not really,' Sakuma replied, and washed down the rest of his cheeseburger with a vanilla shake.

By *everybody at your place* he meant the people I live with in the two-bedroom apartment in Chitose Karasuyama. And snide old me was trying to force him to tell me the name of the person he was interested in, namely Kotomi Okochi – Koto – who'd been watching the rerun of A *Nurse's Work* and trimming her split ends.

'I'm not trying to screw with you, but I'd give up on Koto if I were you.' I reached out for some of Sakuma's leftover fries as I said this, a warning I'd given him any number of times.

'That isn't bothering anybody, is it? Me waiting for her to break up with her boyfriend?'

Sakuma tried to slurp up some more of his vanilla shake, but the straw scraped around on the bottom and he came up empty.

Koto has a boyfriend. Or at least she thinks she does. (Now, this is unclear and would only confuse an innocent guy like Sakuma.) Koto is more than pretty, she's drop-dead gorgeous. This isn't just my personal, self-righteous view, either. If she were standing in front of us right now, I bet most guys would admit it. And this stunning girl sits every single day, in self-imposed confinement in our apartment, decked out in a tracksuit. It's all the fault of the guy she's gone out with since junior college, an up-and-coming young actor named Tomohiko Maruyama (who right now is starring on TV in a romance with the model-turned-actress Ryo Ekura, playing her younger lover). Koto sits in the living room from morning till night, waiting impatiently for him to call, which he does once a week, sometimes not even that often, occupying the rest of her time by trimming her split ends and sometimes diligently indulging in her hobby of making sweets.

'Hey, do you mind if I stop by your place tonight?' Sakuma was trying to sound casual. By now we'd left the Lotteria and were heading towards the pool hall.

'Okay with me. You never give up, do you?' I laughed.

'It's not like I'm going to tell Koto how I feel or anything!'

'I see – you're going to do it again?'

'I told you I'm not!'

'You forget what happened last time?'

'I remember. But I was just, you know, trying to drop a hint, and I guess I went too far . . .' Sakuma said, embarrassed. As he stepped over the railings, he banged his shin.

'So that's how you just drop a hint? Looking right at her and saying *I love you, Koto. I think about you all the time. And it hurts so bad when I do . . .* Some hint.'

'For me that's kind of indirect, yeah.'

'And what did Koto tell you after that?'

'I don't remember.'

'Want me to remind you?'

'Okay.'

Koto had just sat there, with eyes down, as Sakuma confessed his love for her. To the casual observer she seemed to be taking him seriously. Before long Mirai Soma (the other girl who lives with us) shouted out from the bathroom, 'Koto! You can take a bath before me!' To which Koto shouted back, 'Hold on! We'll be finished here in a second.' She was definitely not interested.

No matter how happy-go-lucky a guy he was, Sakuma went home discouraged. I felt sorry for my only friend and confronted Koto. 'Even if the way you acted was just a product of your *psyche*,' I told her, 'the way you treated him was awful.' *Psyche*, by the way, means 'the unconscious', and is a term Mirai started using all of sudden after she read a comic book version of Freud's theory of psychoanalysis. It's become a buzzword around our apartment.

1.2

I did some occasional squats as I stood there in the convenience store, reading my fill of magazines. Finally I ran out of things to read so I started looking through *Cosmopolitan*, where I happened to run across a short interview with Tomohiko Maruyama. I decided to buy it as a present for Koto. In the interview Maruyama said, laughing, 'When I like a girl I want to be with her all the time. I'm very possessive that way.' Considering what a possessive boyfriend she has, it's amazing that Koto still finds time to never miss an episode of *A Nurse's Work*.

The convenience store is right in front of the building we live in. When I left the shop, I waited for a break in the traffic and crossed the road. Inside the lobby of our building I saw that the lift was under maintenance, so I took the emergency stairs instead. As I got to the landing on the second floor I heard somebody above me, sobbing.

So I wouldn't surprise whoever it was, I clomped loudly up the stairs, humming. I rounded the corner up to the fourth-floor landing, and came across a high school girl sitting there on the stairs, in her school uniform, her feet quite pigeon-toed. She was clutching a handkerchief to her face, which was the same level as mine as I stood on the landing. It was too narrow to just squeeze by without a word, but I wanted to avoid what happened the other day when I ran across another girl like this and spoke to her and was told in no uncertain terms to get lost. The girl this time, though, unlike the other sobbing girl, had a normal-length skirt and hair that wasn't dyed.

'Um, I wonder if . . .'

I wonder if you'd let me by, or *I wonder if you're okay*. My opening left it fuzzy which one I meant.

The girl looked up from her handkerchief, startled for a moment, and hurriedly stood up. The book bag on her lap slipped off, and crashed to my feet. As I picked it up I asked, hesitantly, 'Did, uh, something happen?' The girl snatched the bag away, said, 'It's nothing,' and she tried to push past me to go downstairs. On a sudden impulse I grabbed her wrist. I had such a tight grip that after trying to break free she gave up, her arm going limp.

'Actually I saw another girl like you the other day – she was crying on the stairs. You went to apartment 402, didn't you? I live next door, in 401.'

When I said apartment 402, the girl's face instantly tightened. I looked directly into her eyes and said, 'If there's anything you'd like to talk about, I'd be happy to . . .'

The girl's eyelashes were wet with tears and their dampness made them look thicker, and longer. I slowly released my grip on her wrist and in a small voice she murmured, 'It's okay.'

'But what about—'

I was growing more insistent, but she quietly replied, 'It's okay. Really. I'm the one who decided to come here, so there's nothing you can do.' With her skirt fluttering as she ran, she sped off down the narrow staircase. I was on the verge of pursuing her, but thought she'd just respond with another *get lost*. So somehow my feet wouldn't budge.

I went back to the apartment in a foul mood. Now Koto was in front of the mirror, plucking her eyebrows.

'Koto, I saw it again.'

'Saw what?' She turned around and her eyebrows were definitely an uneven thickness.

'Apartment 402 . . .'

'An old guy? Or a young woman?'

'A young woman. Actually just a high school student. She was on the stairs, crying.'

'Hmm. Sometimes the girls cry when they leave, but others seem happy enough. I guess there are all kinds . . .'

'How can you be so blasé? The apartment next door is a brothel, for God's sake.'

'We don't really know that, do we?'

'Listen, a sleazy middle-aged guy lives there. And other middle-aged guys who look like they have money come there, and young girls who look like they don't have any. What else could it be but prostitution?'

'Well the girl I saw said *Thank you very much!* and politely bowed. You think a girl engaged in prostitution says *Thank you very much!* and bows when she leaves? I think it's some kind of weird religion. Best not to get involved. If it turns out to be Aum, then what? They'll kill us.'

I went to the kitchen, opened the fridge and saw a glass bottle with iced tea in it.

'Koto, did you put this in here? Can I have some?' I was already pouring it out into a glass.

'You'd better not. That's not mine, it's Naoki's. It's jasmine tea or something he brewed up this morning.'

When I heard that it was Naoki's – Naoki Ihara is one of our roommates – I poured it back in the bottle. Knowing Naoki, he probably drew a line on the bottle so he'd know how much he'd left.

'Has Naoki said anything? About 402?' I asked Koto's back as she continued to pluck her eyebrows.

'He said, "Well, what about us? We live like we're in a commune, or like illegal aliens, without telling the management company. We're in the same boat.'"

'Illegal aliens?' I muttered and poured some flat cola into a glass.

Why am I living a communal life like this? It's hard to explain, and I don't really feel like trying. Lots of people, including my friends at college, have asked me why. The more I try to explain it, the more it feels like I'm getting further away from the real reason. I asked Koto the same question once. 'Why are you living here with everyone, Koto?' I asked. Her answer was simple: 'Because Tomohiko lives in a company dorm and I can't live with him.' In other words, for Koto there are only two choices: *Living with Tomohiko Maruyama* and *Everything else.*

Our apartment is laid out like this: there's a bathroom on the right as you come in, then you go down a short hallway where there's a kitchen on the left. This isn't one of those dinky half-kitchens that you find in a studio apartment – it's generous enough so you could easily gut and clean an entire tuna. Next to the kitchen there's a sliding door, which leads to the guys' room, an eight-mat Japanese-style room that Naoki and I are sharing. Naoki sleeps on a loft-style pipe bed, while I sleep on a futon below, on the tatami. There's a desk, but we all use it for ironing and it's cluttered with spray starch and a misting bottle. A sliding glass door leads out from the guys' room to the balcony. It's not too small, but not big enough to make you want to do some gardening or put in a wood deck or anything.

Go back to the kitchen and slide open the glass door, which doesn't slide open easily, and there's the large living room. The south side is all windows and it's a little noisy with the traffic from the Kyukoshu Kaido Boulevard below, but it's a sunny room and when Koto hangs out her underwear, it dries in an hour or so. As I said, Koto spends almost every day in the living room. She has a mobile so she could get Tomohiko's calls anywhere, but she insists that the chances of him calling are greater if she stays put. (I have my doubts . . .) An awful light-purple fake leather sofa and a glass table round out the living room.

Beyond the living room is a slightly smaller Western-style room that the women occupy. It isn't off limits to the guys, and when we get together to drink we often use their room, especially since Mirai likes to stretch out when she drinks. Mirai sleeps in a double bed, while Koto, like me, prefers sleeping on the floor in a futon. This is where the four of us live.

I was sitting on the sofa in the living room, finishing up the flat Coke, when I remembered the copy of *Cosmopolitan*. 'Here you go,' I said as I handed it to Koto, who was still engrossed in plucking her eyebrows.

She seemed to have already read it, and flipped through the magazine without much interest. 'Oh, yeah,' she said. 'Someone named Umezaki called.'

'You mean the Umezaki from my club? What'd he want?'

'I don't know. He asked whether you're going on the trip with him or not.'

Umezaki, who is a few years older than me and used to be in my club at college, had invited me to join him on a weekend trip to Izu Kogen. A couple that was supposed to join him had backed out at the last minute and, with no one else to invite, he'd phoned me and suggested I join him, and bring a girl along.

'Are you free next weekend?' I asked Koto, whose face was all scrunched up as she plucked her eyebrows. As I expected, she said, 'As long as Tomohiko isn't going to call me.'

'When will you know if he's going to call?'

'By next weekend.'

'You mean when next Saturday and Sunday are over you'll know?'

'Yeah . . . I suppose.'

'I don't know how you put up with it. Waiting so patiently every day for him to call you. Don't you ever think you're wasting your life?'

It wasn't like I was dying to take Koto with me to Izu. It's just that if she didn't watch what she was doing, she was going to wind up with no more eyebrows.

'Of course I do,' she said.

'Really?'

'Yeah, really. I mean I'm the one stuck here all day waiting for the phone to ring.'

'See what I mean? But you're pretty calm about it.'

'Of course.'

Being that calm is pretty scary, I think. A woman you supposedly broke up with waiting for ever for you to call. All the while calmly plucking out her eyebrows.

'So can you go?' I asked.

'Go where?'

'Oh, that's right . . . Umezaki invited me to go with him next weekend to Izu Kogen.'

'Have I ever met him? On the phone he said "It's been a while," and I was thrown for a second.'

'You remember – he's the older guy in my club who brought over the washing machine.'

'Oh, yeah – that kind of intellectual-looking older guy?'

'That's him. Anyway, that older, intellectual-looking guy's asking us to join him on a trip next weekend to Izu Kogen.'

'Izu Kogen? What're you going to do there?'

'I don't know . . . tennis, maybe?'

'Play tennis, with this intellectual guy, in Izu Kogen?'

'Yep. Interested?'

'What do you think?'

'I didn't think so.'

Koto had tweezed out enough eyebrows, but still went back to plucking. Like she wanted to make absolutely sure the right and left eyebrow were perfectly even. I gave up on inviting her, rolled up the *Cosmopolitan* I'd wasted my money on, and stood up. 'Anybody drying clothes on the balcony?' I asked.

'I don't think so . . . You going to do some laundry?'

'Um. You have anything you want me to wash?'

'Yeah, I do.'

Tweezers in hand, Koto scurried over to the bathroom. As I was going into the guys' bedroom she thrust a balled-up toilet seat cover at me.

'This? All right. I'm not going to use any fabric softener. Is that okay?'

I obediently took the seat cover, went into the guys' bedroom, closed the door, and flung the seat cover as hard as I could against the wall.

1.3

I was watching the pink toilet seat cover and my underwear and shirts sloshing around in the dirty water of the washing machine, when for some reason I thought of Shinya.

Etsuko, who'd been a classmate of mine from junior high and was in the same basketball club in high school, had phoned me a month ago. 'Oh, by the way,' she said, 'did you hear? Shinya died.' She'd called because Disney Sea had just opened and she and Noriko and Risa, also from the basketball club, were planning a trip to Tokyo and thought we should get together. After we caught up on various news she said, 'I'll call you again when our schedule's set.' She was about to hang up when she came out with that *Oh, by the way* and told me about Shinya's death. She was so casual about it, like she was reporting that her neighbours had built a fence or something, that at first all I could manage in response was a simple, 'Really?' According to Etsuko, Shinya had died in a motorcycle accident that just involved him. 'You weren't that close to him at all, were you?' Etsuko said, and I let it go at a simple, 'Yeah, you're right.'

Shinya and I were classmates in junior high. I think it's the same in most schools, but you could divide the boys in our class into four groups. You have the clear-headed brainy ones who sit in the first row, then the jocks who sit behind them and doze off in class (that's the group you could mostly find me in). Then in the seats next to the hallway are the members of a subculture or the science nerds who, during break, would get all excited talking about Bruce Lee or pro wrestling. Then finally there are the bad boys, including Shinya, who sit in nice sunny spots near the window.

I don't have any recollection at all of enjoying talking to Shinya at school. All I recall is we were both big fans of the actress Naoko Iijima and he forced me to buy a photo book filled with pictures of her.

Occasionally I'd spot him, out of his school uniform, in the shopping district in town, and it was hard to imagine him shouldering a regulation school backpack. He looked more like a gang member who'd just done time in jail.

But just after the summer holidays in our last year of junior high, this classmate I hardly knew randomly called me.

'Hey, how you been?' Shinya said.

What do you mean *how you been?* I thought. Didn't you just see me in class today? 'Uh, yeah. I'm fine,' I managed to reply. Had I done something to offend him enough to pick a fight with me? Was it going to be like in a TV drama where he'd force me to meet him behind our school building, or on an embankment next to a river? I started to imagine myself as some bullied kid.

'You free today?' Shinya asked. He sounded almost embarrassed.

'Uh – what's going on?' I asked, still totally convinced I was heading for a beating.

'No, I was just thinking, like, if you're free, you could come over and we could hang out at my place . . .'

Hang out with him? I didn't get it. Maybe *hang out* was some kind of code word? I stammered something and Shinya said, 'Yeah – I'm not sure how to put it . . . but you're studying for the high school entrance exams, right?'

'Ah, yeah. Sort of . . .'

Our conversation was finally sounding like something you'd expect between junior high students, and I felt relieved. I still couldn't figure out why he called me, but at least it didn't sound like he was going to take me behind the school and beat the crap out of me. He repeated his invitation to hang out and I didn't have any excuse not to go, so I said okay, hung up, and rode my bike over to his house.

When I got there and went up to his room, the first thing that took me by surprise was the strawberry shortcake and tea set out nicely on a table. He'd apparently done this for me. I looked at him, seated there, and noticed he had no eyebrows. There was an awkward silence for a while, and then the words that came out of his mouth startled me even more than the strawberry shortcake. 'Could you help me study?' he asked.

I was really surprised. I asked him to repeat himself a few times, and though the way he said it grew more rough, going from *I'd like you to help me study* to *Help me study* to *Come on! You've got to help me!*, the message remained the same. Shinya was telling me he wanted to go on to high school. *I don't know anyone else I can ask*, he added.

After that day I used to stop by his house a few days each week, after school. He'd sworn me to secrecy about the tutoring – I wasn't supposed to tell anybody else in our class where I rushed off to after school. The rumour started to spread around the basketball club that I had a girlfriend. Things got blown out of proportion to the point where they were whispering things like *I hear she lives in the next town over and is as ugly as sin*.

Honestly, I didn't feel like teaching Shinya, and besides I wasn't that great a student to begin with. I kept going to see him because he wasn't as bad a guy as he looked. Actually the more we talked, about how much we liked Naoko Iijima, among other things, the more I realised how well we got along. Every time he invited me, I was happy to go over to see him, and we'd just sit there, talking about all kinds of crazy things until his parents yelled at us from downstairs to be quiet. We never touched the textbooks spread out on the table. After a while, I started hanging out at his place even when he hadn't called me. Shinya enjoyed laughing at all kinds of random crap, and I'd never imagined how seriously he was thinking about his future. His natural gentleness helped him get along well with others, but this proved a handicap, making him fall behind everyone else, and I think he was truly trying to get his life together. I was just a normal, healthy junior high student, son of the owner of a small sushi shop, and I couldn't imagine that anyone like him was such a mess.

In the end Shinya didn't even apply for the high school he had hoped to attend. 'No way I could get in, even if I took the test,' he explained. I wanted to insist that he should at least try and take the exam, but it wasn't even clear that I'd be able to get in either. So I was pretty sure my pupil wouldn't make the grade.

Shinya wasn't stupid. If our classmates hadn't studied at home or attended after-hours cram schools – if they just took tests based on what they learned at school – I think he might have had better grades than anybody. But life isn't that easy. Like the race between the tortoise and the hare, the tortoise doesn't win because he plods along, doing his best. He wins because he doesn't let the hare see him plodding along.

After I graduated from junior high, my relationship with Shinya suddenly came to an end. But we'd always kept it a secret, so from the outside it looked like nothing had changed.

The last time I saw him was the week before my high school graduation ceremony. (I was the only kid from my junior high who passed the exam and attended that high school.) I ran into him on the bus. We hadn't seen each other for a long time, so we had lots to catch up on. 'Next month I'm going to Tokyo,' I told him.

'Wow,' Shinya said, a little envious. 'That's great, man – you're going to be a college student in Tokyo.' As his stop drew near he stood up and started towards the exit, but stopped, like he'd forgotten to say something. 'Hey, keep it up,' he said. 'Let's face it, I'm a screw-up and I'll probably stay that way. So be a success for me in Tokyo, okay?'

For a month after I received Etsuko's phone call about Shinya's death, this picture of his accident raced through my head at night, when I was trying to fall asleep – even though I never witnessed it. In my mind, Shinya is speeding down a straight road on his motorcycle. Maybe there's something in the road that he swerves to avoid and he loses his balance. But knowing him, I'm sure he would have been able to right himself. Even if he did wipe out, I just couldn't imagine him dead. He was athletic, and handsome. He could beat the track team guys at sprints, and our music teacher, an old maid, used to say he looked like James Dean.

When we met on the bus Shinya had also told me about a prank he had played on my father.

'You know that huge house across from ours? The Yanagawas'?' he asked me. 'When I was in grade school, me and some of my friends called your shop and said, "This is the Yanagawas on 3-chome. Please deliver four orders of your best sushi right away." It was raining like crazy and your dad's raincoat was soaked when he arrived on his motorcycle. The rain was coming down so hard that your dad was squinting and his face looked kind of scary. We were peeking through the curtains, giggling, never thinking we were doing anything bad, just that your dad's face looked funny all wet like that. We were a bunch of brats. Your dad parked his motorcycle in front of the Yanagawas' and he ducked inside through the side entrance. We waited to see what sort of expression he'd have on his face when he came out. After a while, I don't remember how long, he came out again, bowing repeatedly and he stooped down through the low side entrance, just like when he came in. We'd thought he'd leave right away. I was sure he'd realise it was a prank call and he'd get pissed off and go home. But your dad, in the pouring rain, started walking around, checking the nameplates on all the houses. He trudged around, getting even more drenched, checking the houses one by one to see if there was another Yanagawa family in the neighbourhood. After a while he finished one circuit of the neighbourhood and came back to his motorcycle and then headed down another alley. I couldn't watch any more and we drifted away from the window, sat back down under the kotatsu foot warmer, and forced ourselves to talk about something else, anything to keep us from thinking about what was going on outside. It was really cold that day, and I don't know how long your dad continued to look for the house.'

My dad. The same dad who took me to the airport on the day when I set off for Tokyo to go to college, so anxious I could barely breathe. 'I know this sounds old-fashioned,' my dad said to me then, 'but find a good older student you can be friends with at college. A mentor. Someone you can be friends with for life, someone you respect.'

'No way do I want to be someone's minion,' I said, laughing.

'You dummy,' my dad said, lightly poking me in the head. 'A person with a good older colleague to take care of him will have good younger colleagues who admire him.'

So I found Umezaki, who gave me the washing machine I was now using to do my laundry. When Umezaki was delivering the machine I said, kind of maliciously, 'If you're going to give me a washer, you should give me a better one.'

'You got a lot of nerve, you know that?' Umezaki replied. 'I'm giving you this for free, plus I brought it over in a truck.' As always, he smiled as he spoke.

The washer he gave me, the kind that has a separate spinner for drying, vibrates so much that it shimmies from one end of the balcony to the other end. The balcony is slightly tilted, too, so water will flow towards the drain. By the time the water's all drained out the washer's pulling at the cable like a dog straining to be free of its leash.

Recently I feel like I want to tell somebody about Shinya. What kind of person he was, what kind of possibilities he had hidden away . . . What kind of life he had, how he died . . . The things he told me on the bus . . . I want to tell all these things to somebody. But right now I have no one to tell. No matter how good a friend Sakuma is, it's not something I can talk about with him. If I did, he'd just make fun of me and then suggest we go shoot some pool. If he did take me seriously I know it would only embarrass me and I'd shut up. Plus I don't want my room-mates – Koto, Mirai and Naoki – to see such a sentimental and serious side of me. Our living arrangement works precisely because we avoid those situations. Life goes smoothly with us because we limit ourselves to acceptable topics, skipping what we'd really like to talk about.

As I waited for the washing to finish, I looked down again at the street below. Maybe because I'd been absorbed in my own thoughts, I hadn't noticed till now the expensive black Century parked in front of our building. The sun had set long before, and the street lights were reflecting in the shiny black body of the car, glistening like an insect. I turned around and saw that the rinse cycle was finished.

It was just then I heard the front door bang, and Koto, looking pale, barged into the guys' room, a bento dangling from one hand.

'What's the matter?' I was standing there, inexplicably holding out my newly washed underpants, fresh out of the wringer, as she, seemingly worked up about something, inexplicably took them from me without a word. 'H-he's here,' she said, her voice shaking. 'He's come to see the people next door.'

'*He?* Who're you talking about?'

'You know – the guy who's on TV all the time . . .'

'Who?'

'I don't know his name. The congressman from Shizuoka or somewhere, the one who's on TV a lot. The guy who was a flunky of that former prime minister, the one I didn't like. The one who's always grinning – *you know* . . .'

'I don't know who you're talking about!'

'I told you, I don't know his name. The one whose face looks like the comedian Knock Yokoyama. You know who I mean . . .'

'Yoshio Noguchi?'

'Yes! That's the guy! And he's come to visit apartment 402.'

I tried to calm her down, and gently guided her into the living room, the damp underpants still clutched in her hands. I gave her a glass of water to drink and sat back to hear her story. She'd gone out to buy a bento at the station and when she got out of the lift and was walking down the hallway, suddenly the door to 402 opened and this guy who appeared to be Yoshio Noguchi emerged.

I thought again of the shiny black car parked outside, but knowing Koto's reaction to the sexual harassment scandal the bald-headed Knock Yokoyama, nicknamed 'Octopus', had been embroiled in, which was enough to put her off eating octopus for ever, instead I pretended to have my doubts.

'Are you sure it was Yoshio Noguchi?' I asked.

'Absolutely,' Koto said, shivering. 'We've got to report it. We've *got* to! When I think of a pervert like that doing who knows what to girls on the other side of this wall, it makes me so sick I won't be able to sleep!' She was outraged.

'Hold on. Weren't you just telling me that they weren't a brothel but some kind of religious group? Telling the police is fine by me, but then they'll check us out too – and if the building's management company find out, then what? They'll kick us out. This building's supposed to be for newly married couples.'

'If it's for newly married couples, then why is a pervert like that visiting?!' Koto looked surprised by her own outburst. She clearly found the idea of prostitution going on next door less disgusting than the thought of a middle-aged pervert frequenting it.

'I've lost my appetite,' she said, and gave me the Karasu bento that she'd gone all the way to the station to buy. For the record, the Karasu (crow) bento is the most popular item at a bento shop in front of the station. *Kara* stands for *kara-age*, fried chicken nuggets; *su* is a dialect pronunciation of the first part of *shoga-yaki*, ginger pork. Both of these are included in the bento at the bargain price of ¥580. The way they flavour the ginger pork is out of this world, and unless you get there before eight p.m., they're usually sold out.

1.4

What's the matter with me? Ever since I came back from Izu Kogen, I feel like I can't breathe. I blame it all on Koto, for not coming with me. No – blaming her won't get me anywhere. I knew from the start that she wouldn't go, and I'm the one to blame for going on the trip that Umezaki had organised, a double-date trip, even though I didn't have a date. Initially I'd turned him down. 'I don't have anyone to go with, so I'd better not,' I told him. But Umezaki, kind as always, said, 'Well, then you should come alone. It's a four-person cottage, and I won't be able to find somebody else at such short notice.'

Someone with more sense would have said, 'No, I don't want to be a bother,' and turned him down. But not me. Instead, I said, 'Really? Then I guess I'll go. I've got nothing else going on.'

We drove to Izu in Umezaki's car. Unlike Momoko, his Pajero's engine doesn't conk out every ten kilometres. It was too much trouble, he said, to come all the way to pick me up, so I drove Momoko to Nishi Kokubunji, parked in front of his building like usual, and blasted my horn a couple of times.

Umezaki's girlfriend, Kiwako, who was going with us, had apparently spent the night at his place. Normally Umezaki would come out on the balcony, but this time Kiwako appeared. She held her hair as the wind blew it around and she gazed down at me like she was inspecting potatoes at the grocery store. I stuck my head out of the car window and bowed, and Kiwako seemed momentarily startled and then hurriedly bowed back. Anybody would be taken aback if potatoes started greeting you. It looked like she was talking to Umezaki back inside the apartment. I wasn't sure if I should go upstairs or wait there in the car.

Kiwako came downstairs with Umezaki to the car park. When our eyes locked for the first time, I admit that I was immediately attracted to her. You could even call it love at first sight. Okay, well, it was my first time experiencing it, so honestly I don't know if that's really what people call *love at first sight* or not. If love at first sight means that when you're with that person you get all restless, more than restless – you're as jumpy as a video tape on fast forward – that you overanalyse each and every word that comes out that person's mouth so when she just says something like *You want to go for a walk?* you suddenly jump to conclusions and are about to call your dad and tell him you're getting married – if all that's what the world means by *love at first sight*, then I think that yes, I had fallen in love at first sight with my loveable older friend's girlfriend.

Unfortunately, when we arrived at Izu Kogen, it was raining. The tennis court we reserved was soaked, and with no hot springs at the cottage, there was nothing else to do. While we waited for the barbeque that was going to be held under the covered terrace, the three of us took walks around the cottage, invaded the soaked tennis court and, umbrellas in hand, batted a squishy wet tennis ball around with our hands. You're probably imagining that Kiwako stood by watching, with a quiet smile on her face as these two mischievous guys dashed around in the rain, but it was actually Kiwako who ran around the most, getting all muddy. She even shouted at me to pick up the pace.

Covered in mud, we went back to the cottage, and, after the evening barbeque, we again found ourselves at a loose end. We took turns taking a bath in the tiny bathtub, and opened a bottle of Chablis we had chilled in the fridge. One beer was all it took for Umezaki to turn into Gushiken, the light flyweight champion. Beer and an oolong tea highball and he'd be Guts Ishimatsu. Add wine to that and he'd leap right over Carlos Rivera and wind up like goofy Tako Hachiro. He knew how he reacted to alcohol but still he drank, so he had only himself to blame. Not that I was entirely blameless myself – I knew what alcohol did to him yet I encouraged him. Predictably, by ten p.m., Umezaki had crashed and was snoring up a storm in the bedroom. Kiwako and I stayed in the living room, with the fireplace that we had been told was off limits. We sat at each end of a three-person sofa, laughing occasionally as Umezaki's thunderous snores wafted out from the bedroom.

Kiwako always referred to Umezaki as *that guy* . . . I don't know how many times that night she used that term. But every time she started out saying *You know, that guy* . . . I called him by his last name. It was a great chance for me, the two of us all alone at last, but all we talked about was Umezaki. It was like he was sitting there on the sofa in the space right between us.

It's been a week since we came back from Izu Kogen. I tried to put that night in the cottage, the two of us alone, out of my mind, but I can't stop thinking about it. I keep replaying the details, wondering why I said certain things, telling myself that next time I'd say something different. All the while knowing that there most likely won't be a next time.

Talking to Kiwako that one night convinced me that the kind of man she's really hoping for isn't someone like Umezaki. Maybe the two of them might even split up. There's a reason I say this: he has zero amount of interest in Kerouac and Boris Vian. Instead he's the kind of guy who doesn't mind telling you that he's seen *Rocky III* five times.

I'm sure Kiwako's aware of this. And I think Umezaki himself feels uncomfortable with who he is. It's just that the two of them can't bring themselves to talk about it. And I'm not just saying this because I secretly love her. I mean, take the other day, before our trip, when he brought the washing machine over to my place. I hadn't met Kiwako yet. When I said, 'How's it going with your new girlfriend?' he said, 'Yeah, we're getting along. I don't know. It's just that . . .'

'Just what?'

'It's just that – she's kind of aggressive. Kind of wild, I guess . . . She comes right out and tells me she wants to give me a blow job.'

I turn twenty-two on my next birthday, but I've never met a girl yet who's said she wants to give me a blow job. Umezaki had filled me in on Kiwako: how they're the same age (in other words, three years older than me); how she's from Sapporo and works for a temp agency that also contracts with the big food manufacturer where Umezaki is employed; and how she lives in a condo in Daita, in Setagaya, with her younger brother, a college student. When I finally met Kiwako, though, she seemed like the exact opposite of a girl who went around offering blow jobs.

Since we came back from Izu Kogen I've called Umezaki's place three times.

'How are you?' I asked.

'You again?'

'Yeah, I didn't have anything else going on.'

'Why are you calling?'

'No particular reason. Do I have to wait until I have a reason to call?'

Umezaki gave an innocent *ha-ha-ha* laugh. I don't think I'd ever called this much except when I wanted something. My motives were pretty obvious, but my naive older friend didn't pick up on it at all. 'How's Kiwako?' I asked. 'She's fine,' he replied. 'You're all she talks about since we came back from the trip.' His total lack of malice made me feel even worse.

Almost every day this week when I recalled our trip, I let out a huge sigh. That night on the sofa, I should have told Kiwako how I felt, and I regretted not doing so. To tell the truth, I felt confident. I'm sure she sensed how I felt about her, and I don't think she would have turned me away if I'd admitted it, but, coward that I was, I avoided letting her know my feelings and talked instead about neutral topics like college memories I had about Umezaki. In return I listened quietly as she talked about her relationship with Umezaki. I wasn't hesitating so much because of him. If I had, for instance, been lucky enough to kiss her on that sofa, I knew it would only make me feel awful. If I had casually let slip an *I think I love you*, it seemed like she would just as casually have slept with me. Even now, a week after we came back, fear of that keeps me plagued by these wimpy thoughts, and unable to take a step forward.

What I'm trying to say is, I don't want to be the one Kiwako cheats on her boyfriend with. Not that I can ask her to break up with him. So here I sit, unable to see her, and going nuts because of it. I don't know what the hell to do.

Suddenly I noticed a knock at the door. I lifted my head from where I was slumped over the desk and there was Koto at the door to the guys' room. Before my trip to Izu Kogen, we'd been all worked up over the goings-on in apartment 402, to the point of considering infiltrating the place, but after I came back from the trip I didn't care any longer what went on next door. Koto, too, seemed able to leave it alone, as long as no bald pervert showed up again.

'What's up?' I asked sullenly.

'Nothing, really,' Koto said. 'You haven't come out of your room in a while and I was wondering what you're doing.'

'Just thinking over some things.'

'Thinking, huh?'

Koto came inside, came around behind me and started massaging my shoulders.

'What are you doing?'

'Well, I was wondering if you'd like to go to karaoke with me.'

'I told you I've got things to think about!'

I brushed her away and when I looked up, Koto seemed worried.

'What do you want?' I asked.

'They asked me to. Naoki and Mirai.'

'Asked you to do what?'

'To take you out for karaoke, and make sure you sang to Shogo Hamada.'

'Why? Why would they want you to do that?'

''Cause . . . you know, it's true . . .'

'*What* is?'

'Well . . . that the person who's having a breakdown is the last one to notice it . . .'

She must be talking about herself. Mirai and Naoki must have said something like *Instead of holing up in the apartment waiting for the phone to ring, why don't you go out and do karaoke?* and she mistakenly thought they were talking about me.

As Koto left my room I heard her yell, 'I have cash, so don't worry. And one more thing: those clothes you've been wearing for a week stink, so why don't you change? And while you're at it, take a shower, okay? That would make me even happier.'

1.5

Last night Ryo Ekura finally broke up with Tomohiko Maruyama. In the TV drama, I mean. I knew from the beginning that she was going to get back together with the popular actor Toshiya Ozawa (who, like her, had started out in modelling), but when Maruyama was sitting there in a restaurant in the posh Daikanyama district as she dumped him, it upset me. Koto was sitting next to me as we watched the show and I said, 'Ryo Ekura has lousy taste in men.' She waited until there was a commercial and replied, 'No, it's the writer who has lousy taste.'

'You got that right. The writer has no sense of reality.'

'Maybe he wasn't popular when he was young, so that's why he always writes this kind of storyline?'

Koto and I had taken quick bathroom breaks during the ads and had settled down nicely once more on the sofa in time for the drama to begin again. Truth be told, TV dramas are pretty boring.

'Sugimoto-kun! *Su-gi-mo-to-kun!*'

An angry voice from behind me snapped me out of my daze.

Ayako, the waitress in charge, held a slip in her hand and was glaring at me.

'Stop spacing out! Did you hear the order I told you?'

'Oh – sorry. I was thinking about the TV show I saw last night . . .'

'TV show? Are you kidding me? I need an enchilada, a taco with cheese and beans, and we're out of limes for the Coronas.'

Just then a customer called out from behind her and Ayako, still glaring at me with a scary look, called back, 'Coming! Just a second!' She sounded like husky-voiced actress Reiko Ohara dubbing in *The Exorcist*.

I've been working part-time as a cook in this small Mexican restaurant in Shimokitazawa for the past eight months. Of course, when I went for an interview I wasn't looking for a job as a cook. My father may own a sushi restaurant, but I don't know the first thing about cooking. And the owner wasn't about to give a job as cook to a guy who was surprised to find that peppers had seeds in them. I'd gone to that neighbourhood hoping to buy some second-hand clothes, but when I saw the 'help wanted' poster, I leapt at the chance. I started off as a dishwasher and waiter, but two weeks into it, the cook, a guy named Masaharu, quit. I knew he and the owner didn't get along, but I didn't expect him to quit so abruptly. And I was the one who got dragged into it. 'You've watched him cook while you were washing dishes, right?' asked the owner (who obviously didn't set much store by the culinary arts). Suddenly, I was in charge in the kitchen. The following week they finally found another cook (who'd worked until the month before in a Chinese restaurant!), but he was into triathlons and demanded three days off per week, including Saturdays. Saturday is the busiest day in Shimokitazawa, so I wound up continuing on as cook. It amazed me that people came in waves to this little Mexican restaurant, with its Chinese-cuisine-trained triathlete cook, and a second cook who had to consult a cookbook and hadn't yet graduated from college.

By the time I finish the last order and clean up the kitchen, it's usually past eleven p.m. That night, I gathered all the rubbish, took it out to the wheelie bins, and had a cigarette, though I don't normally smoke.

When I got back inside, Ayako had taken her hair down and was sipping a Tecate, and going through the receipts. I took off my cooks' uniform and said, 'We were really busy today. We must have made, what, ¥100,000?' Ayako silently shook her head. Sometimes the owner shows up just as we're closing up, but usually it's Ayako who takes all the cash and deposits it in the bank's night deposit box.

'Can I give you a ride back to your apartment?' I asked her. I sat down beside her. Ayako sings in a rock band, and works at this restaurant to make ends meet. She's turning twenty-nine this year, and I don't know if it's supposed to be serious or a joke, but her band's name is Limit.

'Oh, Ayako, there's something I wanted to ask you.' I was helping her total up the profits for the day and she looked at me, irritated.

'What?'

'A hypothetical, okay? You have a boyfriend, right? If a younger friend of his told you he loved you, what would you do?'

'What do you mean, what would I do?'

'I mean, would you be upset, or happy about it?'

'Does that younger friend have guts?'

'Guts? Not so much, I'd say.'

'Then I'd be upset.'

'Really?'

'I would be if he said *I love you.*'

'Well, okay. But what if he *had* guts?'

'Hmm . . . Does this guy listen to The Who or The Kinks?'

'I don't think so.'

'Then he's more into the Sex Pistols or the Clash, that kind of music?'

The name of her band, Limit, probably wasn't a joke after all.

We left the restaurant and I drove to her apartment over on the other side of the station and then drove back to Kannana. Normally taking the back streets through Sasazuka and coming out onto Kyukoshu Kaido Boulevard would be fastest, but these past few days I've been intentionally driving through Kannana, even though it's so crowded. Go into a back alley a little way from Kannana and there's the apartment where Kiwako lives with her younger brother. According to Umezaki it's a one-bedroom, and Kiwako uses the bedroom while her brother sleeps on the living-room couch. Usually there's no light on in their place. Or at least the light's never been on since I started driving past here after work. Umezaki told me that the brother has a girlfriend in Kashiwa City in Chiba and he basically lives there. Tonight, I gazed up sorrowfully at their dark window, assuming that Kiwako was at Umezaki's.

I parked Momoko behind the building, got out, and headed towards the entrance. The entrance has an auto lock with a video intercom. I waited across the street, smoking a cigarette in front of the vending machines, until a guy in a suit, and no doubt drunk by the way he staggered, went into the building. He punched in the door code and as the door clicked open I followed him in, trying to look like I belonged there and just happened to show up at the right moment. The man apparently lived on the ground floor, because he didn't take the lift, instead heading down the hallway. I was watching him when he suddenly turned around. I nodded to him, and the man snorted a little laugh, and reeled down the hallway again.

I took the lift to the third floor. I'd come this far before. But each time I hadn't made it to the apartment itself. The first time I came here, I just stood in front of the apartment building; the second time I touched the mailboxes outside the entrance; the third time, thanks to a woman who was going out, I made it inside; and the fourth time I actually took the lift before I turned around and left. Tonight was the fifth time and finally I was standing outside Kiwako's door.

The nameplate read *Hiroshi and Kiwako Matsuzono*, as if they were a married couple. I pressed my ear to the door but couldn't hear anybody inside. I thought about last night, when I went into the girls' room at home. Koto was already lying on her futon. I sat down formally, with my legs tucked under me, and confessed. 'Every night, after work,' I said, 'I wander in front of her apartment building.'

Koto looked really sleepy, but for once, she took me seriously. 'That's awful,' she said. 'You're acting like a pervert.'

'You think so?'

'You need to realise it yourself.'

'Realise what?'

'That you're acting like a pervert.'

Okay, so if I realise I'm acting like a pervert, then what? I decided to tell her more.

'I really think I like her.'

'You like her? Or you *think* you like her?'

Of course Koto was hung up on details.

'I said I *think* I like her because I'm a bit shy about it.'

'On the outside you seem pretty naive, Ryosuke, but you're more complex than I thought.'

'I seem naive?'

'Well, that's what Mirai and Naoki say . . . Anyway, you should stop moping around outside and ring the bell and tell her how you feel.'

'But what should I say?'

'Tell her *I think I like you. The* think *part is 'cause I'm shy.*'

'Confess how I feel? No, I can't do it,' I said, sighing. 'I mean, she's Umezaki's girlfriend.'

'Then there's nothing you can do,' Koto said, and rolled over to go to sleep.

She didn't know the first thing about giving love advice. The one thing you should never advise the person is to tell the truth. Mirai, who was lying in the bed, grumbled, 'Could you guys stop whispering in the dark like that? I'm trying to sleep here.'

I ignored Mirai's complaints and went on. 'I know she feels something for me. But maybe to her I'm just someone to have a fling with.'

'Why don't you ask her?' Koto said sleepily.

'What should I say?'

'How about—'

That's as far as I heard, because then I was smacked with a pillow.

'Unlike you two, I have to get up for work in the morning!' Mirai yelled, so, obediently, I left. Through the closed door I could hear Mirai saying wearily, 'Christ. All you guys think about is love affairs.'

So, here I was, on my fifth try at seeing Kiwako. I was clinging to her door, my finger pressed against the peephole, when I heard the lift behind me slide open. I spun around and there she was. I could tell she was surprised. She stood there, unmoving, her eyes gliding from my face to my shoulders, to my finger plugging up the peephole.

'Wh-what are you doing here?' she asked.

'What am I doing? Well, I, uh . . .' I answered.

Kiwako slowly walked towards me. She looked different from when we were on the trip, probably because she was wearing a suit.

'My brother isn't back yet?'

'Uh . . . no . . . not yet.'

'You came to see us?'

'Yeah, uh . . . that's right.'

'What's going on?'

'I just happened to be in the neighbourhood . . .'

That was the exact line I had told myself *not* to say if we did run into each other. Smiling, Kiwako stepped in front of me and unlocked the door. Inside, a phone was ringing.

1.6

It's been thirty minutes now. I've been sitting in classroom 534 in the main building at college, in the last row, gazing at the blank blackboard. I'm alone in the room. The rows of desks all slope towards the blackboard, so from the very back row, it looks like large waves of long, neatly lined-up desks are pushing towards the podium. And I'm riding the crest of this wood-grained monster wave.

I think it was really hard for my parents to send their son to a private university in Tokyo. When I was a kid my mum always used to say, 'Running a sushi shop is a respectable profession. But your father hopes that you'll become the kind of customer this kind of restaurant values, rather than running the restaurant yourself.' Since coming to Tokyo, I haven't once been to a sushi restaurant. Kaiten sushi places and the like, yes, but they don't count.

Women always strike me as much more realistic than men. At first my mum was dead set against me attending a private university in Tokyo. Part of this was simply because she's a mother – because she wanted to keep her only son nearby. But then she carefully read through the information pamphlets on colleges, as well as the book I bought on living in Tokyo, and began estimating what it would cost for her son to attend college there. Naturally, for the wife of a sushi restaurant owner, this was a fair amount of money.

When Mum told me how much it would cost, I kind of half gave up. Since I was taking the scattergun approach, applying to a lot of places and hoping I might just get accepted somewhere, the exam fees alone started to snowball, in inverse proportion to my indifferent academic record. The more exams, the more we'd have to shell out for hotels; and even if I were to pass, I'd have to immediately cough up entrance and tuition fees, plus all the other endless fees, as well as rent for an apartment. When my mum showed me how much it would all come to, an image sprung into my mind of my dad making mounds of chutoro sushi to pay for all this.

My mum's apparently implacable opposition was undone by a single sentence from my dad. She didn't tell me about it until later. He said, 'If he wants to go to Tokyo then we should let him.'

Mum replied, 'That's sounds good, but . . .' and showed him the estimate, enough to strike fear into anybody's heart.

But Dad ignored it. Instead he said, 'Let's think about you, first of all. Your friends are all from this backwater town in Kyushu, right?'

'That's right,' she said. 'They're people I went to school with in junior and senior high.'

'Same with me. Ryosuke should go to Tokyo and meet all kinds of other people. Don't you think so? Like, say, the son of a guy who fishes for bonito in Tosa, or the son of an old established restaurant in Kyoto, or the daughter of a dairy farmer from Hokkaido. He should make friends with all kinds of people like that.'

Mum didn't say anything. She told me later that while she listened to him she was already making a preliminary mental list of what I should pack when I moved to Tokyo. Finally, according to her, Dad said the following:

'Fathers are different from mothers. The only thing fathers can do for their sons is give them a kick up the bum to send them out into the world.'

As I stared vacantly at the blackboard, the door adjacent to it opened, and a young guy stuck his head in. When he spotted me in the last row he said, loudly, 'Hey, isn't this Marketing Theory?'

'No,' I yelled back. I'd seen this guy before. We sat next to each other in the cafeteria once, and he gave me a copy of *Spirit* magazine that he'd finished reading.

'Damn. Got the wrong room.'

He was about to leave when I told him to wait.

'Hm?' he said, reluctantly turning around.

'This is going to sound strange, but what does your father do for a living?' My voice echoed around the empty classroom.

'My father?'

'Yeah.'

'Why?'

'No special reason.'

'He's a civil servant.'

'Where?'

'In Kanazawa, in Ishikawa Prefecture.'

The guy looked puzzled for a moment, and then left. But I thought to myself, *Dad, I just met someone whose father is a civil servant in Kanazawa.*

I checked my watch. I still had time before my part-time job started. I could take Momoko for a drive around the city, but these last few days, whenever I drove her, it made me increasingly depressed. It wasn't especially complicated – it brought back memories of the other day, when I was stalking Kiwako on the way back from work and before I knew it was in her apartment.

It was Umezaki who was calling when she entered the apartment. She'd given me a little shove and I was already inside. As she talked to him she motioned with her finger for me to help myself to a drink from the fridge and to sit down. I sat there, waiting patiently for her phone call with Umezaki to end.

When she hung up, I suddenly realised something very important. I was sitting right in front of her on the sofa, looking like some hand-me-down cat – no, more like one that's been handed down *several* times – yet Kiwako never told Umezaki that I was there. *So there's still some hope,* I thought, convinced I was right.

'You didn't tell him I was here,' I said, avoiding her eyes.

She took a carton of Sunkist grapefruit juice out of her shopping bag. 'Did you want me to?' she asked, shooting me a meaningful glance.

'I don't really care if you do. I mean, we both know him, and it's not like we're hiding anything . . .'

Kiwako totally ignored what I said. She was absorbed in stowing away the juice and some fruit in the fridge.

The living-room sofa had a pillow that smelled of some kind of hair gel, probably her brother's, and a crumpled-up blanket. A white door stood ajar at the edge of the room, leading into what appeared to be Kiwako's bedroom. I could see a shelf lined with cosmetics, and a framed poster for the French film *Sam Suffit*, a film I'd seen at Mirai's recommendation, propped up against the wall.

'Oh, that's right. On the phone just now, Umezaki said *Say hello to Ryosuke for me.*'

'Huh?' Before I knew it, I'd leapt up from the sofa.

'Just kidding,' Kiwako said, and came out from the kitchen.

'He wouldn't know I'm here.'

'I guess not.'

When I'm with Kiwako it's like I have to play the part of the sweet younger guy, and afterwards it makes me want to throw up. I'm not the sweet type to begin with, and trying to pretend I am is asking too much. I'm aware of all this, but in moments like these, I still overdo the younger guy act.

To cut to the chase, that night I slept with her. We had some beers and chatted a bit about Umezaki, and afterwards it was like a totally natural thing for us to wind up in her bedroom. As natural as finding Koto in the living room trimming her split ends, or Momoko conking out after ten kilometres.

The girls I live with, Koto and Mirai, are kind of eccentric. But being with Kiwako, who is so different from them, made me feel peaceful. I decided, without much of a reason, that it's because she's from Hokkaido. But that can't be right – not all people from Hokkaido are like that. Take the owner of the restaurant I work at – he's as thick and oily as a bowl of butter-pork ramen.

At any rate, I love Kiwako's voice. When we snuggled in bed I was suddenly aware of how tiny she was – so tiny that I could hold her tight in my arms. I told her to say something, anything, so she whispered something against my chest. She laughed – what she'd said was 'On your mark, get set, go,' but her breath was hot against my chest, gently filtering up to my neck. 'Consider this for a second,' Kiwako said. 'A film – a love story – about a man who doesn't mind sleeping with his older friend's girlfriend, and the girlfriend who doesn't mind sleeping with her boyfriend's younger friend.' I wished she hadn't said that. I couldn't think of a smart comeback.

'Ryosuke, are you tired?'

'Huh? What did you say?'

'Nothing. I was just wondering if you were sleepy.'

'I could sleep. Once I close my eyes I'm out like a light in five seconds.'

I'm not sure how much I caught of what was going on, but if social hierarchy is fixed, I'm most definitely the lowest class of all, the one that's exploited and not given an ounce of respect.

When I woke up the next morning Kiwako wasn't there. I found my underpants, which had slipped into the crack between the bed and the wall, tugged them on and padded out to the living room, where I found a guy I'd never seen before buttering a slice of toast. As I stood there wondering whether I should go into the living room in my underwear or go back to the bedroom, the guy glared at me sullenly. Just then Kiwako emerged from the kitchen, a coffee cup in each hand.

'Morning.'

She smiled a perfect morning smile and set one of the cups down in front of the guy. 'This is my younger brother, back after a night out. Looks like he's a bit pissed off about me bringing a man home with me.' She smiled again.

Her brother was shoving a fried egg on toast into his mouth, and I nodded a greeting to him. Be friendly and the other person will do the same, sort of. At least he no longer looked like he wanted to kill me. I hesitated, then came out into the living room dressed only in my underwear. Kiwako and I had shared a bed last night so I was going to sit down beside her, but I felt her brother's icy stare. Younger brothers apparently have special feelings when it comes to their older sisters. Feeling strangely apprehensive, I sat down next to her brother instead, which made the situation even stranger. As I sat down beside him, her brother glared at me even more coldly. Kiwako looked at her lover and kid brother, side by side.

It was after this, though, that I totally lost it. Seated beside her brother, I was eating the toast she'd made for me, slathered with butter and jam, washing it down my parched throat with some chilled orange juice. In front of me, Kiwako was sipping her hot coffee, beside me her brother silently chewing his toast. And that's when it happened.

'Ryosuke. Are you – crying?'

Until Kiwako asked this, I didn't realise I'd been crying. Her brother looked dumbfounded.

'What the heck is he crying for?' he asked.

'Wh-what's the matter?'

It was definitely creeping them out. You're enjoying a bright, sunny morning, eating buttery, slightly burnt toast and drinking hot coffee when, out of the blue, the young guy sitting there in his underwear starts blubbering.

'Sorry – I'm sorry.'

I had no idea where these tears were coming from, but I tried my best to stop them. But still the salty tears kept rolling down, dripping down beside my nose to my mouth as I chewed on the slice of toast.

'Man . . . this – is so weird,' I stuttered.

The more I tried to casually explain it, the more my voice broke, until I was on the verge of sobbing. Kiwako hurriedly passed me a tissue. Her kid brother's mouth was wide open. He looked at me like he was ready to make a run for it.

But for some reason, while I was sitting there eating the toast Kiwako had made for me, I had pictured my father's face. He was getting things ready in the sushi shop, and the shop was full of the smell of vinegary rice. And then I saw Shinya. Shinya as he was getting off the bus, patting me on the shoulder and waving and saying, 'Hey, do your best there in Tokyo . . . be a success for me, too, okay?' As I drank down the orange juice I desperately tried to shake off this mental image. The next face I saw was Umezaki's, as he brought over the washing machine to my place.

'I'll be on the sofa, watching TV,' he'd told me, 'and Kiwako will kneel down between my legs. And I'll say *I like this way the best*, and she'll say *Me too*.'

As he struggled with the heavy washer, Umezaki gave an embarrassed smile.

Then I remembered some words Kiwako and I had exchanged in bed the night before. Our bodies were flushed and I was holding her tight.

'I like this way the best,' I'd said.

Breathing against my chest, Kiwako said, 'Me too.'

I went on crying. The tears wouldn't stop. It was like there was another me, totally separate, ignoring the real me, and crying like crazy.

2.1

The daytime TV show *It's Okay to Laugh* is amazing. I can watch it for a whole hour, but as soon as I turn off the TV, I can't remember a single thing they said or did. It's the definition of the word *pointless*.

I switched off the TV and was sitting there wondering what to have for lunch when Ryosuke emerged from the guys' bedroom. His eyes were sleepy, his hand was inside his underwear, and his hair, as always, was a mess. Seems like he tosses and turns most nights. Naoki, who shares the room with him, said if the room didn't have walls, Ryosuke would probably roll all the way to the station.

'Ryosuke, what do you want for lunch?'

Ryosuke took a carton of milk out of the fridge. He sniffed at it, then started drinking. He motioned for me to wait and, with his neck stretched out, drained the carton.

'How about you, Koto?' he asked with a burp, and I stared for a moment at his white milk moustache.

'How about KFC?' I asked back.

'KFC? What about that new soba noodle place that opened in front of the salon you go to? Why don't we eat there?'

He stuck his right hand down his boxers again and scratched, then drifted off to the bathroom. He's in the middle of an *unrequited love* for the girlfriend of his older friend Umezaki, but these past few days he hasn't mentioned it at all. The other day, uncharacteristically, he stayed out overnight. I asked him where he was, and he did say At *her place* – but for a first-night stay with a girl he didn't seem all too thrilled by it. Maybe he'd already had his heart broken. Anyway, I don't care about the *casual affairs* of a guy like him. He might be torn between the demands of love and friendship, but clearly he's not losing any sleep if he can sleep enough to have cowlicks like that, so I'm not too worried about him.

Five months ago, when I moved into this apartment and first met him, the thought struck me that the hiragana symbol *fu* described Ryosuke perfectly. It wasn't like he was slumped over, the way the symbol looks, it's just that when I looked at him, the negative prefix pronounced *fu* always came to mind. *Fuantei?* (*Un*stable?) *Fukigen?* (*Un*happy?) Or is it *fushigi?* (*Un*usual?) No, that's not quite it. *Fu, fu, fu* . . . *Funuke?* (*Un*assertive.) That might be closer to it.

When Ryosuke came out of the bathroom I asked, 'Which character is used to write the *fu* in *funuke?*'

Without washing his hands, he grabbed a cookie off the table. 'The *fu* in *funuke?* It's something to do with internal organs, or guts or something, isn't it?' he said, chomping on the cookie. 'Like you have no guts.' I pictured Ryosuke's body, all hollowed out, and the cookie he was chewing swirling down inside this body, like falling snow.

Ryosuke apparently had nothing going on until the evening, when he went out to his part-time job. It had broken my heart to do so, but I'd finally switched off the TV (I'd started out watching the morning talk shows and somehow had kept on watching all the way through *It's Okay to Laugh*), but as he contentedly chewed on his cookie, he turned it on again. A talk show had started and the expressionless face of the host, Baku Owada, appeared. Whenever Ryosuke turns on the TV these days it always starts zapping. 'Not again,' he muttered and he started to hit the left side of the set. 'Not there,' I quickly cautioned. 'Hit the right side, three times,' and he did as instructed. But the static remained.

'It doesn't work.'

'You're hitting it too softly. You've got to hit it hard, hard, then soft. You have to get angry with it.'

'I can't be angry with a TV. Koto, you try it.'

'No way. I just turned it off.'

As we bickered, the clear picture returned, all by itself. Ryosuke changed the channel with the remote and said, 'Who's the guest on *At Home with Testuko* today?'

'What do you have planned for the afternoon?' I asked Ryosuke, who ignored the TV now and headed back to the guys' bedroom. 'I going to wash Momoko,' he said happily. 'I envy guys who get all excited about washing their car. They probably don't have a care in the world. They're probably so carefree they go looking for problems.' On the TV Emiko Kaminuma's cooking show was on and she was preparing a spring chicken with aromatic spices. It looked delicious.

I'm keeping it a secret from my parents that they (Ryosuke and Naoki) live in this apartment. It's not like I'm ashamed of it or anything, it's just that they don't need to know how their supposedly level-headed daughter is living. Far from being ashamed of living with Ryosuke and Naoki, I'm more ashamed at how little there is going on between us. Of course, when I first started living here, the way Ryosuke would casually check out my breasts felt like a hot arrow. I learned from watching the women who run those shooting galleries at hot springs resorts that when the arrow misses the target, the best thing to do is to pull it out right away and hand it back to the customer. The customer isn't stupid, and if you pull the arrow out right away he understands that he missed. Still, there are plenty of women in the world who go around with arrows still stuck in them. So the customer's left waiting for his prize, which causes all sorts of problems. There are too many women running shooting galleries who are unmotivated – women who, with countless arrows sticking out of their chest, complain about *not being able to make any men friends* as they grab away the money from the half-drunk guests.

I think the reason I'm okay with living here is that my room-mate, Mirai, isn't one of those women. Of course another reason is that Ryosuke and Naoki aren't like the policemen and civil servants who go to hot springs resorts and go totally nuts.

Coming to live here happened all of sudden. Like a bolt of lightning. Or more like a bite on the backside by a dog. No, not really . . . Anyway, one night five months ago I was dancing at this club I liked to go to when the music stops and the lights go on. The guy dancing in front of me is all sweaty, and I'm all sweaty, and the DJ hurriedly announces, 'Sorry, guys, we're having problems with the speakers, so please be patient,' and the people around me laugh or complain, and everyone staggers off to the bar. The guy in front of me asks if I'd like a drink, and that's the instant it hit me, like a revelation: *I have no interest in anything.*

I don't mean no interest in immediate things, like that sweaty guy or that there was nothing I particularly wanted to drink. I noticed I didn't have any interest even in the kinds of things that my family liked – my father and his job, teaching maths in a local girls' high school, Mum and her housework, my sister and her volleyball team, my other sister and her infatuation with Shingo Katori, one of the singers in the group SMAP. As I found myself alone there on the dance floor, the revelation startled me. I hadn't asked for it, but at that instant the knowledge that I was leading an empty life really hit me hard.

Right after I graduated from junior college, I went to work at the branch office of a pharmaceutical company and got paid at the end of every month by direct debit. I think even then I must have noticed an emptiness, a sadness, deep down inside. Every time I got paid I'd go out to eat at a fancy French restaurant with my friends, or buy a ring at Tiffany's, but these things never really satisfied me. Then I'd go to a bookshop and see a pile of books with the title *It's Okay: Enjoy the Present*, and I'd figure the life I was leading must be fine after all.

It was tough coming to the realisation that I wasn't interested in anything, though realising it didn't mean I could then immediately find something to engage my interest. I tried to think of something. Maybe I could study a foreign language, or study abroad in Rome or somewhere? Or, more realistically, grab some guy I knew and have a destination wedding abroad? But everything I could think of was based on how envious it would make people, not on any genuine interest I might have. Still, in high school, when the boys held a contest to select the prettiest girl, I always came out on top. Which doesn't mean that the other girls hated me or anything – they didn't. I even had girlfriends who, as they started to get a little drunk, would say embarrassing things like, *I envy you, Koto – you're beautiful and such a sweet girl*, to which I'd reply *I don't know what to say!* I was pretty satisfied with being that sort of girl.

And then suddenly, because of the speakers breaking down at a club, I found myself on a brightly lit dance floor, hearing a voice – whether that of an angel or the devil, I don't know – saying *You haven't suffered. So you haven't experienced true happiness.*

'What's wrong?' the sweaty guy in front of me asked and without thinking I yelled out, 'No way!' I wasn't answering him, of course, but this voice in my head that was lecturing me about *suffering* and *happiness*.

The guy looked at me with this *did-I-say-something-wrong?* sort of expression. *Ah! That's right!* I thought. 'Didn't you say your brother was driving a truck to Tokyo tomorrow?' I asked.

'Yeah – yeah, I guess I did.'

'Do you think he can give me a ride?'

'To Tokyo?'

'Right. To Tokyo.'

'What are you going to do there?'

'Suffer.'

'Huh? Suffer?'

'That's right. Suffer.'

The guy looked puzzled, but went ahead and called his brother. After that, though, he avoided me for the rest of the night.

I'd decided I'd go to Tokyo. Tokyo wasn't the main attraction, though. I wanted to be near Tomohiko Maruyama. Loving him was the only thing I'd ever suffered over in my life.

I met Tomohiko at a party soon after I started junior college. We had such a typical first meeting it's almost too embarrassing to talk about. Naturally all five girls who were in the room had their eyes on him. It's kind of slutty for me to say this (but if I think it and don't say it, it's even more slutty) but some of the guys there – okay, I'll go ahead and say it: *every single one of them* – were interested in me. But I couldn't act all innocent, couldn't pretend to be prim or pretend to be surprised at coming out on top in the end as the most popular girl naturally would. So instead I went after Tomohiko openly, right from the start – so much so that the other guys backed off. As the most popular girl I felt I had the right to sell myself openly.

I got a call from Tomohiko the day after the party. The group of people I was with had gone on to a second bar to continue the party, and after that broke up, we girls went by ourselves to a third place, then wound up at a wild karaoke party. Completely wasted, with my throat aching from belting out Chisato Morisato tunes and my stomach aching from too much Bombay Sapphire gin, I stumbled home around five a.m. Tomohiko called me four hours later, just before nine.

On the way to the second bar everyone had stopped by a convenience store to buy gum and disposable cameras, but Tomohiko and I waited outside.

'So, have you always been interested in people's teeth?' I asked casually. Even if the other girls had no shot at Tomohiko, they were staying out past curfew because all the guys in the group were promising catches – they were in dental school. Dentists-to-be.

Tomohiko paused. 'I'm really sorry, but I'm not like the rest of them. I work in a DIY store.'

At that moment I was grateful I'd watched soap operas since junior high, since it helped me come up with a line like something out of one of those shows: 'No need to apologise. I'm just a junior college student myself,' I said, very calmly. A full moon was in the sky, he and I were lingering along the dark road at night. Any second now I expected to hear cheesy dramatic music.

'But all of the others are for real,' he hastily added. 'They're real dental students. I didn't want to come, but Kengo – you know, the one with glasses? – we've been friends since we were kids – he dragged me along.'

'But wasn't it Kengo who introduced all of you? He said you're all in college together.'

'He did, didn't he? It would be embarrassing for me if the truth came out. I'm sorry about that.'

Guys might project this 'we're just innocent boys for ever' look, but deep down, they are totally insecure.

When he called the next morning, I was so hungover I couldn't remember what we talked about. But I was lucid enough to make a date with him, because after I hung up, I found myself clutching a memo that said 7 p.m., Saturday, in front of the Civic Centre.

One thing I noticed when I was walking down the street with Tomohiko was that girls check out guys pretty openly. They'd look at him first, then check out the girl on his arm – me – then look back at him once more. Thanks to Tomohiko, I saw things I'd never seen before. Once I even saw a McDonald's employee so overcome by Tomohiko's good looks that her hands started shaking. *I'd like a takeaway*, he'd told her, but from the way she reacted, it was as though he'd ordered her, not a vanilla shake.

'So you're pretty popular, aren't you?' I couldn't help but say as soon as we exited the store.

'You must be, too, Koto,' he replied, which was nice to hear. Yeah, we were being snide, but whatever. The vanilla shake we took turns slurping tasted delicious.

Around noon, Ryosuke and I went for lunch at the new soba place in front of the station. Ryosuke's hair was still a mess of cowlicks. They were giving a twenty per cent discount on all orders to celebrate the opening, so the place was packed. We were about to give up and leave when a four-person table opened up. The waitress looked a little put out that we were going to take up so much space, but we sat down anyway. When she brought us water she said, 'You might have to share the table with someone else later.' I'd been sitting across from Ryosuke but went around and sat down next to him.

We were eating bowls of nothing-to-write-home-about katsudon when, as the waitress predicted, we were asked to share the table. I looked up and who was standing there but the middle-aged man who lived in apartment 402. His hair was just as it was when I saw him in our building – slicked back with pomade. Who uses that any more? His lips were thick and purplish, the heavy beard on his hard-looking skin freshly shaved. Ryosuke was still working on his katsudon. He didn't look up so I elbowed him in the ribs. He let out a little yelp. 'What did you do that for?' he complained, rice grains sticking to his pouting lips. And then he seemed to take in, for the first time, our neighbour standing there. Ryosuke tensed up. In an attempt to cover it up, he called out to the waitress, helplessly. When she trotted over he quickly gulped down his almost-full glass of water and asked for more.

The guy from 402 was already seated across from us. We'd seen him a number of times in our building so he had to know we were his neighbours, but he pretended not to notice and, with narrowed eyes, studied the menu taped to the wall. Everything about him gave me the creeps, even the way his Adam's apple stuck out. He ordered goshiki soba, the Girls' Day dish – not exactly what you'd expect a man to order. When I thought of how he helped dirty old men hook up with young girls – this guy sitting right in front of us! – I totally lost my appetite. The plump egg in my bowl of katsudon suddenly looked like a wart on the forehead of one of those old lecherous men, the droplets of moisture clinging to the lid of the bowl like sweat, and I felt like I was going to hurl.

I couldn't stand it any more so I grabbed Ryosuke by the arm and tried to pull him up so we could leave. He started to get up, but he looked longingly at the last slice of pork left between his chopsticks and wouldn't let go. The man from 402, engrossed in a copy of *Shukan Jituswa*, a sort of smutty weekly magazine that always featured a pin-up on the cover, gazed up at us with a smirk.

I flung down the money next to the register and we went out. 'Did you see it? That guy's face? *Unbelievable!*' I yelled, not caring if anyone else heard us.

Ryosuke, still chewing a bit of pork, said casually, 'You think he noticed we're his neighbours?'

'Of course he did!' I yelled back. 'And did you see how nonchalantly he ordered goshiki soba! Can you believe him!'

Ryosuke ignored how upset I was and calmly walked on.

I grabbed his shoulder. 'Hold on! It doesn't bother you?'

'There's nothing we can do about it. There's all kinds of people in the world. People who plough fields, people who sing in front of the station, people who sell cigarettes, people who drive the Shinkansen . . . all sorts. So what's so strange about people pimping for prostitutes?'

'How come you're so knowledgeable all of a sudden?'

'Well, Naoki and Mirai said that – that there're women who are happy to sell their bodies . . . Plus, keep in mind that relationships with neighbours in the city can be pretty delicate.'

'But what about that girl you saw crying on the stairway?'

'I know, but there are lots of girls who cry for some reason. At least according to Mirai.'

'Come on – they're running a brothel next door to us!'

'I know, but still . . .'

'Damn, you're making me crazy here! If that's what they're doing, we need to expose them.'

'How are you going to do that?'

'Well . . . You could be a client.'

'*Me*? No way!'

'Why not?'

'I just – don't want to.'

'If you're worried about the money, I'll give it to you. After you figure out what they're up to, then you can make an anonymous call to the police.'

'You'd really give me the money? . . . Nah. I don't want to do it.'

'Maybe you've never been to a place like that before?'

'Never!'

'Why not?'

'How the hell can you ask me that?'

From there our conversation went in a whole new direction. Ryosuke insisted that he would never pay for sex. But we decided that Naoki might – though ultimately we concluded that while he didn't have a regular girlfriend, he often met up with his ex, and probably just took care of business that way. Eventually apartment 402 dropped out of our conversation altogether.

When we got back in front of our building, Ryosuke said, 'I'm going to go wash Momoko. You want to come?'

'To wash your car? Will you pay me?'

'In the end you'll be the one asking to pay *me*.'

He wanted me to tag along, so I decided to do just that. If I went back to the apartment now, I'd have nothing to do. I rode on the back of his bike to where Momoko was parked.

He was right. I ended up enjoying it so much I told Ryosuke to bring me along the next time he took the car to be washed. It was a coin wash, and I found out something I'd never known: car washes have a time limit. Three minutes to rinse the car off, then you soap up and wash the car, and if you slack off even for a second the alarm will buzz to tell you that you only have thirty seconds left. 'Koto! Get that spot over there – over *there*,' Ryosuke instructed me and we were able to wash the whole car. Then comes the final rinse, and this has a time limit, too. I shrieked as my hair and face got soaked, but we somehow managed to finish washing the car. 'If it's this much fun,' I pouted, 'you should have invited me a long time ago.'

Afterwards, we took the sparkling-clean Momoko for two nine-kilometre rides, and got home before five. Then Ryosuke went to work at the restaurant and I sat there as always, fantasising about Tomohiko. The days really do race by.

Five months ago, when I caught a ride in the large truck with the brother of that guy who was trying to pick me up in the club, and landed in Tokyo in the middle of the night, it was Ryosuke, in Momoko, who came to pick me up. The truck driver was much older than his brother, a nice guy around forty with a wife and kids. 'You're lucky you got me to give you a ride,' he said, laughing. 'Some of those other guys would be trying to get it on with you in the back seat by now.'

I phoned home when we stopped at a rest area in Shizuoka. My mother couldn't believe it – the notion that her daughter, who'd gone out to go dancing, had suddenly just hitched a ride to Tokyo to see an old boyfriend was completely bizarre to her. The only thing she said was 'Tokyo?' Then she went silent.

'Tell the office I'm sick or something, okay?' I said.

'When are you coming back?' she asked.

'I don't know yet.'

'What should I tell your father?'

'Can you just figure that out yourself?'

'How can you say that? And are you really in a truck? Not a plane or a train?'

'Yes! I caught a ride in a truck.'

'Hmm . . . a truck . . .'

Naturally when I got out at Tsukiji, I called Tomohiko right away, but nobody answered. I let it ring ten, twenty times but it didn't go to voicemail. I started to feel lonely for the first time and began to cry. And as I was crying, I phoned my one and only friend in Tokyo, Mirai Soma.

'If you're going to cry all over the phone, I can't figure out what you're trying to say!'

Hearing her voice, the same as always, made me happy and I cried even more loudly.

'What?' she said. 'All I can figure out from what you're saying is that a nice truck driver bought you a bowl of kitsune udon in a rest area.'

I explained the whole thing. 'You idiot!' she shouted. 'The trains aren't even running at this time of night, so I'll ask Ryosuke, this guy I'm living with, to collect you in his car.'

I was finally able to get in touch with Tomohiko five days later, after I'd settled down in this apartment. Even if he was just being polite, Tomohiko sounded happy to hear I'd come to Tokyo.

'How come you came all the way to Tokyo?' he asked in his usual cheerful voice.

'I came to see you,' I said, and he burst out laughing.

Once when he used to work at a DIY store, I went to check him out while he was working. He was in the Gardening section, wearing a green apron and gloves, and carrying a potted benjamin out to a customer's car. My chest tightened painfully. It was the first time that seeing a man working had done this to me. As he walked back from the car park, I waved to him from the entrance. He looked a bit put out, but then trotted over and said, 'What's going on? How long have you been here?' It sounded a little forced, but he did look happy.

Tomohiko and I dated for a year and seven months. The DIY store was open 365 days a year, and was especially busy when college girls like me had time off – summer and winter break and other long holidays – and usually he couldn't even get a couple of days off in a row. Still, whenever we could get together, we did.

I knew that he was living with his mother. And I suspected that she had some health issues. The reason I say this is that often, when we were out on a date, he would call his home or the care-taker at his apartment. Plus, no matter how sweetly I tried to get him to stay the night in a hotel, he never would.

Only once in the year and seven months that we went out did he sleep over, and that was when we went to the beach. The place we stayed at was a cheap bed and breakfast that didn't have air conditioning and all night long we had to listen to the owner's baby bawling downstairs. Still, though, I always think that it's because of that one night that I have such strong feelings for Tomohiko.

Ever since I was a child I have believed that you shouldn't bring up a topic the other person avoids mentioning, so I never asked about his mother. But that night, when he said, 'Let's shoot off some fireworks,' and we went down to the beach, I said, 'You know, if there's anything I can do to help out, I want you to tell me.' At first he didn't seem to understand. He was holding a Roman candle up towards the sky, and said, 'What?'

'. . . I mean, with your mother . . .'

At that instant purple flames leapt out from the tube in his hands.

It wasn't until we'd finished with the fireworks and were walking back, arm in arm, towards the bed and breakfast, that he responded.

'The president of the store where I work – the guy who owns the whole chain – has a son who's the same age as me. The son is just nineteen but he drives around in a BMW. Sometimes, during college holidays, he makes the rounds of the stores with his father. The manager and floor chief of our store are these older guys, but you should see how they bow and scrape to the president's son. I guess it's not surprising – happens all the time that employees will fall all over themselves at a company's successor-to-be. But I was thinking, is that really the way things should be? I'm not that smart, you know, and I'm not great at explaining things. And I do know that the president deserves our respect. But the other guy's just his son, so does that really make him great too? I said this to the floor chief once, during a break, and he said, *He's the next president, so of course he deserves our respect!* I supposed he's right.'

I didn't understand what Tomohiko was getting at. I just smelled the sea and held on tight to him.

'Like, take North Korea,' he went on. 'I read in a magazine how the son of Kim whatever-his-name-is went to boarding school in Switzerland. Since grade school, I think. And they sent another boy the same age to be with him and take care of him in the boarding school. Like a medieval retainer. When I read that, I was eating lunch and it sent a chill through me and I totally lost my appetite. This might be a leap, but I was thinking that maybe there's really no reason to bow and scrape to the company president's son. Maybe all these things we take as a given just shouldn't be.'

I pictured a young man in a classroom, expressionless, hurriedly kneeling down to pick up the eraser a boy has dropped. We made our way back slowly to the B&B.

Back in our room, we took turns taking a bath. While I was bathing, Tomohiko went outside to play a trick on me. He was going to peer in from the window to scare me, but the owner discovered him and gave him a good slap across the back with a stick. I heard him scream, 'I'm telling you the truth! That's my girlfriend in there!' so I leaned out to the owner to explain, and to rescue Tomohiko. My face was bright red, not from the hot bathwater, but from the embarrassment of hearing him yell out – so loudly his voice must have carried all the way to the beach – that I was his *girlfriend*.

'My mother worked for years as a housekeeper,' he told me, when he came back inside. 'You remember Kengo? That guy that was with us when we first met? My mum was their housekeeper.'

When Tomohiko quit his job at the DIY store and went to Tokyo, I only found out about it second-hand. This was just after I graduated from junior college. I'd already broken up with him. You could say I ran away from him, but putting it that way is a little misleading. What I ran away from was the circumstances *surrounding* him.

It still makes me shiver to remember the first time I met his mother. She was sitting on the steps of their apartment, nude from the waist down. When Tomohiko saw this, he shoved me aside, raced up to her, threw his jacket over her waist and slowly led her, step by step, up the stairs to their apartment. She'd been sitting outside, vacantly gazing at the moon in the night sky.

I stood there, frozen, not knowing if I should follow after them or turn around and go home. One voice in my head urged me to follow them; yet another told me to go home. I started to panic. Back on the beach I'd promised him *If there's anything I can do to help out, I want you to tell me*, but now what was I meant to do? The half of me who raised her hand then, I'm sorry to say – and I mean *really* sorry – is the half that was afraid and wanted to go home.

He phoned me early the next morning. 'I'm sorry about last night,' he said. 'There's nothing to apologise for,' I told him. But the spell was broken for me. Every time after that – when we went bowling, when we drank a vanilla shake, or even when my younger sister said *You've got a call from Tomohiko* – the image of his mother haunted me. Going out with him meant going out with his mother as well. He's the one who said he wanted to break up, but I'm the one who made him say it. I'd just turned twenty then – I was in college and was just out to have some laughs and a good time. Both the angel and the devil sitting on my shoulders were in innocent, high spirits all the time, badgering me with questions: *Now what? Now what are we going to do for fun? Hm?*

At the earliest, Naoki gets home at nine p.m., Mirai at ten. Naoki works for a small film distributor. He explained what he does once, but it was sort of confusing and I can't say I totally get it. Mirai's job, though, is easy to understand. She works in a store that deals in imported goods, and even takes the occasional buying trip abroad. She insists she just does it for money, and that her real calling is as an artist. I've gone out with her several times when she sells her drawings – she spreads them out on a cloth on the pavement along Omotesando, or at the entrance to Yoyogi Park, and even next to the pond in Inokashira Park.

Compared to Ryosuke, who comes straight home after his part-time job, I'm never sure when Naoki and Mirai will be back. It's not just because they're working late. They're very different types of people, but they both tend to get really drunk. They love to boast about how there's not a street in Tokyo – in Ginza, Akasaka, Roppongi, all the way to Kabukicho in Shinjuku – that they haven't passed out on. When Naoki comes home wasted, he isn't much trouble. He goes to the bathroom and groans and retches for a while, but once that's over, he collapses wherever he is and peacefully snores away. His one problem, though, is what he says in his sleep, which isn't normal. One night I was going to the kitchen to get a drink of water and Naoki was asleep on the kitchen floor, still in his suit. All of a sudden he yelled, 'Watch where you step!' I was sure he thought, mistakenly, that I was stepping on him, so I gently said, 'Don't worry, I won't step on you.' But then he sat up and said, "Cause there's one like – this big,' and he held his thumb and index finger apart.

'Huh? What is?'

'There's one this big there, so don't step on it.'

Naoki looked towards where I was standing, his eyes darting around anxiously, then plopped back down on the floor and shut his eyes. I was the one who was taken aback – what was he talking about? 'Where is it?' I said, hopping about the dark kitchen.

The next morning Ryosuke told me that Naoki often dreamed about a tiny elf. Ryosuke had even heard the spell that Naoki intoned in order to make the elf appear.

Still, compared to Mirai, there's something kind of charming about Naoki's drunkenness. When Mirai staggers home drunk it takes for ever for her to settle down. She doesn't hurl in the bathroom, or pass out on the floor; instead she insists on drunkenly acting out the performance she gave to entertain her friends at whatever bar she happened to be at that night. Needless to say, as soon as she comes home, Ryosuke and I beat a hasty retreat to our bedrooms.

Even if we do that, Mirai will stay in the living room alone, practising, with dance steps thrown in, the song 'Nowhere to

Stay' by Masanori Sera. Somehow she just isn't satisfied with the performance – I don't know what aspect of it doesn't meet her standards, but nobody knows that song nowadays anyway, so who cares?

Despite all this, I like living here. It's fun, though there is a fair amount of tension in the air that comes with living with others. But I especially like the fact that, should my situation change, I can move out at any time. If I told them I'm moving out tomorrow, I don't think any of them would complain, and even if Mirai left, I think at this point I could stay on.

To put it another way, take the world of online chat rooms. I'm hopeless with technology and try my best to avoid it, but according to what my friends from junior college tell me, our life here is kind of like living full-time in a chat room. The main reason I don't use the Internet is, like I said, my complete ineptness when it comes to technology, but also, if I could be completely anonymous then I might say something totally cruel. And if I feel that way, so does everyone else . . . and then we'd all be backstabbing and wasting time. So no thanks. Still, my friends tell me that not all sites are so evil. They say there are some where you can actually open up in a real way. These seem to be sites that are *full of goodwill*. Places where you can unload about your problems and be sympathetic, maybe even encouraging, towards others, and get the same in return. If, on occasion, someone shows up saying something nasty, the others respond with something like *I've gone through some tough times, too, so let's all hang in there* or *Thank you. You're absolutely right*, which then provokes someone to write something like *Heh, heh, heh – you want to suck my cock, don't you?* which, naturally, everyone else totally ignores. This is a space where only those of goodwill can enter, and you're free to come in or out any time.

That's all a long way of saying that this apartment we're living in is the same sort of space. If you don't like it, all you have to do is leave. And if you stay, you've got to be happy. We're human beings, so of course there's a mix of goodwill and hatred in all of us. I think Mirai, and Naoki and Ryosuke, are all trying to put on a good face. We're definitely what you'd call *superficial acquaintances*. But for me, this is perfect. I know I can't live like this for ever, but for now, it works, and is meaningful, because we know it's temporary. Turn on the TV and all you see is people snapping at each other. Open up the newspaper and you read about people trying to snatch away the rights of others. Or talk with friends and it's all about a scramble over men . . . Honestly, I'm sick and tired of every kind of hatred that exists between people, the hatred that fills the world. Whether I'm sick of it or not doesn't make hate disappear, of course, and some people might laugh and say I'm wearing rose-coloured glasses when it comes to reality. But I'm tired of those naysayers too. I'm tired of all of it.

2.2

I was jolted out of a deep sleep by one of those noisy campaign trucks blasting out election slogans – this one for a Democratic Party candidate named Toyoko Fuchino. I haven't officially changed my residence to Tokyo so I can't vote here, but if I could, I'd write in *Anybody but Toyoko Fuchino*. Having any interest in an election, of all things, must mean my days have become more dull and monotonous than I realised.

I went out to the living room in my pyjamas and the door to the bathroom swung open and there was a guy I'd never seen before, with a bath towel wrapped around his waist. I was startled for a second, but then I figured it must be one of Ryosuke's friends from college. 'Good morning,' I called out, and he said, kind of shyly, 'Oh. Good morning.'

It was almost ten a.m. This morning, it must have been after four, I remember Mirai stumbling in, wasted as always, groaning something about *Never again. No more drinking! No more dancing!* Then she stepped over me and collapsed in her bed. Despite what must have been a pounding hangover, she seemed to have got up and left for work.

The boy was standing there passively, his hair all wet, and I said, 'If you're looking for the hairdrier, it's over there,' and pointed to the shelf. I opened up the door to the guys' bedroom, but the two of them had already gone out.

'Where's Ryosuke? At college?' I turned around and asked the boy.

As he tugged at the drier, he replied, 'Uh – yeah. He left about an hour ago.'

'You don't have classes today?'

'Classes? Me? No.'

'Then let me ask you something. Do you have plans today?'

'Plans? No, not really . . .'

'Then why don't you stay here until Ryosuke gets back?'

I could tell he was wary, as if I were going to bite him.

'No? You want to go home?'

'No . . . it's all right.'

'Really?'

'Uh, yeah.'

'Great. I tell people I'm not bored, but it does get kind of stressful being alone here all day.'

The words poured out of me suddenly, as if I was possessed, and the guy looked at me with this *Well, why don't you go out sometimes?* look on his face. Ryosuke apparently hasn't told him yet how I spend my days.

Anyhow, I made a fresh pot of coffee. Before he went to work, Naoki must have made and drunk his banana protein drink, because there were dirty cups and stuff piled up in the sink, so I quickly washed them and then made myself some toast and eggs. The boy got dressed while I cooked. He asked me what he should do with the wet towel, and I told him to shove it in with all the other dirty clothes in Ryosuke's overflowing laundry basket.

As he sipped the fresh coffee – like it was something extra-ordinary, like he was a young boy holding a prized *kabuto* beetle for the first time in his life – the guy talked about the hectic interactions he'd witnessed in the living room this morning.

'I was sleeping on the couch and about seven, I think, that door opens and a guy comes out and he's all, *Who the heck are you?* and when I tell him *I'm Satoru* he asks *Is anybody using the bath-room?* and before I can answer he goes inside. When he comes out he comes over and says *What day of the week is it? . . . Hey, this tie doesn't go well with this shirt does it? . . . Oh! Turn on the TV – the Fuji channel. The astrology corner's starting . . .* I'm trying to sleep here, but he's so loud I'm completely awake by now, my head throbbing from an awful hangover, but I give up trying to sleep and get up. *Got a hangover?* he asks me. *Banana juice will cure that.* He whipped up a batch with that juicer over there. But banana juice the morning after you get wasted? I told him I was going to puke if I drank any.'

'You didn't know Naoki was living here?' I asked as I topped up our coffees.

'I didn't. I thought I was alone. And after that guy forced me to drink some banana juice, then *she* came out.'

'Mirai?'

'Right. Mirai. That was awful. She had a worse hangover than me – actually it was more like she was still drunk. She pointed at me and she's all *Who are you?* and I'm all *I'm Satoru!* And though she's the one who asked she gets all upset and says *So what? You don't have to get all huffy about it!*'

'And then both of them left for work?'

'Yeah, they did. Naoki's all, *This is Aries' lucky day!* And then he left. Mirai soaked in the tub for like a half-hour and she let out these screeches every once in while that startled me and I went over to the door and asked her if she was okay, and she's really calm, she's all *This is how I get the alcohol out of my system.* While this was all going on Ryosuke came out, looking like he'd woken from a horrible nightmare. As soon as he spots me he's all *I'm just an awful person . . .* And I'm all, *Say what?* He looked so tormented I had to look away. When Mirai comes out of the bath she's all, *Give me a ride to Harajuku, Ryosuke* and it seems like it was too early for Ryosuke to go to college so she says, *I'll fill up Momoko's tank next time,* and just after nine, I guess, the two of them left.'

What Satoru described was simply life as usual. A typical morning in our living room.

'After they left I figured I could get some more sleep, but I just couldn't so I took a bath. And when I finished, you came out,

Kotomi, and yours was the first decent *Good morning* of the day. How many people live here, anyway? Is somebody else going to show?'

'No, that's it,' I said, laughing, as I stacked our yolk-stained plates.

I took a shower and then I took Satoru to a pachinko parlour in front of the station. Recently I've started to believe – for no reason whatsoever – that if I win at pachinko, Tomohiko will call me. But Satoru was the one who was really into it, way more than me.

On the way back to the apartment, we had mint chocolate chip ice cream at Baskin Robbins. Then we stopped by a convenience store so that I could check the new issues of *Anan* and *Junon* to see if there were any articles on Tomohiko when suddenly Satoru says he's got to leave soon. If he left, I'd be all alone till evening, so I said, *Hey, why don't we play* Biohazard 2 *back at my place?* And I convinced him to come along.

And that's when, for the first time in eight days, I got a phone call from Tomohiko. Pachinko got me excited but, I mean, this is above and beyond. He said he wanted to see me! After I hung up, without thinking I hugged Satoru, who was standing behind me. When I hugged him I caught a whiff of this weird smell coming from his neck. It wasn't a sweet smell, nor was it a sharp, citrusy smell either. An unusual smell, like sweat and dried dirt.

He seemed really surprised that I hugged him. When I explained that I would finally get to see my boyfriend, because he now has a little free time, Satoru managed a smile.

'Gl-glad to hear it,' he said.

I dressed in a rush, making sure my make-up was just right, and went out to the living room. 'I'll go with you to the station,' he said, getting up from the sofa. I felt bad since I'd invited him to play *Biohazard 2* with me, and for a minute I'd actually forgotten he was still there.

'Ryosuke should be back soon, so why don't you wait here?' I said, half apologetic.

He looked a little unsure. 'It's okay. I'll go with you.' He was studying me intently.

'What is it?' I said.

'You really look better in those kind of clothes, not a tracksuit,' he said, which made me happy.

We took the Keio Line from Chitose Karasuyama and got out at Shinjuku, where we said goodbye.

'Drop by again sometime,' I told him.

'Really?' he said happily.

'Next time we'll play *Biohazard 2* for sure.' We smiled at each other and parted ways.

Usually Tomohiko and I meet up in a small hotel in Ebisu. His dorm is a five-minute walk from there, in Higashi 3-chome in Shibuya-ku. What I'm trying to get at is . . . okay, it's hard for me to put it in my own words, so let me just quote Mirai, 'A call girl's got a lot more sense – at least she gets money for it.' It's true. With Tomohiko's crazy schedule, we can only spend a short time together in a hotel, and the only thing we can manage is *that*. Time is always tight because of his work, so everything's limited – there's only so many minutes to take a shower, so many minutes for foreplay, so many minutes for you-know-what. I always wind up calculating each segment of our time, and I'd be lying if I said that Mirai's suggestion of a call girl didn't cross my mind. 'I mean, a popular actor asks his former girlfriend to come to a love hotel with him, right?' Mirai had argued. 'Saying he has a sudden opening in his schedule.'

Okay, I see her point, but I'm no call girl. Even if Mirai insulted me, saying I was some kind of 'new type of call girl' who didn't do it for money but for love, I'm confident enough to tell her she's got it totally wrong.

First of all, no man introduces a call girl to his colleagues and bosses. I've had dinner three times with Tomohiko and his manager, at the home of the husband and wife who own the management agency. The husband's a dead ringer for Tony Tani, the skinny vaudevillian, while his wife looks just like Chikage Ougi, the actress-turned-politician. Naturally Tomohiko introduced me as his *girlfriend*. The couple pretended not to hear this, but afterwards when the wife and I were washing up in the kitchen – she cautioned me to be careful with the dishes – *They're Wedgwood, you know!* – she told me that she'd heard a lot about me. 'Tomohiko,' she went on, 'refers to you as his *soulmate.*'

Can any man treat his soulmate like a call girl? Not likely.

Another reason he meets me in a hotel, not in his dorm, is because his mother lives with him. I call it a dorm, but actually it's just a regular apartment. Until six months ago another would-be actor lived with them, but then Tomohiko made his splashy debut before his roommate had much success. So the roommate got all huffy, like a girl, and moved back to his home in Kishiwada. So now it's just Tomohiko and his mum living there. If I hadn't met the owners of the agency I would have found it pretty remarkable that he had brought his sickly mother to live with him in this talent agency's company dorm. But knowing now what kind of people the owners are, and how much Tomohiko trusts them,

I can sort of understand how he decided to try to make it as an actor in Tokyo.

The owners of the agency, this older couple, had their eyes on Tomohiko from the time he was attending his all-boys high school. Even back then he was attractive enough to knock the socks off a girl behind the counter at McDonald's with a single smile. So it wasn't strange that the head of a talent agency got wind of this knockout high school boy – even though this was in a city far from Tokyo.

Sadly, Tomohiko's mother's condition has grown worse in the last few years. At the hospital they diagnosed it as severe manic depression brought on by the menopause.

'When she's feeling good, she's the best mother in the world,' Tomohiko told me. 'Makes me wonder how someone could be such an amazing mother. But when she's ill, it's like I feel I have to be the best son in the whole world.'

Thanks to the kindness of the couple who owns the agency, his mother goes to the hospital once a week where she receives counselling from a specialist, and all other necessary treatment. When Tomohiko's out on a shoot, a staff member from the agency stays over at the apartment to take care of her, and to make sure she keeps her doctor's appointments.

'I have to make it now,' Tomohiko told me, laughing, 'or else they'll always be in control of my life.' He'd already found the people he'd wanted to stake his life on, the ones he could share the joys and sorrows of life with, and it made me a little envious.

He never takes me to see his apartment, no matter how many times I've asked. I don't feel like saying anything crass and insensitive any more like 'If there's anything I can do, just let me know.' The girl I was before, always just looking for a good time, ran away like a coward from him. Now I think I should face the reality of the situation as it is and accept it, but not with some arrogant attitude about wanting to help. When I ask him to let me see his mother, he says, 'If I get dumped again, I won't recover.' He's joking, but it makes me feel like killing myself. But I don't tell him I'm sorry for what happened. I know if I do, he'll have to forgive me for acting so stupid then.

'Why are you willing to see me again?' I said this on our second date after we met again in Tokyo, when I'd finally worked up the courage to ask him this.

'Why?' He paused. 'Because I still like you. When you called me and said you were in Tokyo, it made me so happy.'

'Even though we broke up like that?'

'Like what?'

'You know . . .'

'You mean when you saw my mother and ran away?'

I didn't say anything.

'Ever since I was a kid I haven't trusted people who put on a good front when you first meet them. I think the same thing applies to the entertainment world.'

He smiled, seemingly embarrassed by how he'd become the kind of actor who plays the handsome, leading man.

I said goodbye to Satoru at Shinjuku Station. When I finally arrived at the hotel in Ebisu it was two hours after Tomohiko had called me. I asked for the room number at the front desk, then took the lift to the room, irritated by how slow it was. I knocked and knocked at the door, but nobody answered so I went back to the front desk and had them phone the room.

I hadn't seen Tomohiko in seventeen days and I think he must have been exhausted and fallen fast asleep on the bed and not heard me knocking. The pattern of the lace pillowcase was pressed into his cheek. The last time I had seen him, he'd told me that he was about to record his first single, called 'Mud' (a title which I was sure wouldn't lead to sales). His schedule was packed, every minute of every day, with things like a promotional photo shoot for the CD cover, magazine interviews, appearances on late-night radio programmes, and meetings to plan out his appearance as supporting actor on his next TV drama.

And yet in the midst of this tight schedule he'd managed to call and tell me he suddenly had half a day free. I don't care what Mirai, Naoki, or Ryosuke say – Tomohiko isn't making time for some cute announcer, and he hasn't made a move on any of his fans. I'm sure of this not because I'm convinced that he's saving himself for me. It's because of his ridiculous schedule. With all the appointments he has, plus time for taking care of his mother, there was no time left to watch porn, much less have an affair.

We hugged, and kissed, and wasted no time jumping into bed. We still had our clothes on, but I could tell that Tomohiko's penis was ready for me. 'Ready for action, aren't you?' I teased, and he replied, a little shyly, 'I'm kind of tired.' I appreciated his honesty, but wished he would have just said how much he'd missed me.

'What's your role in the new TV show?' I asked as I undressed and got under the covers.

'It's a baseball player who injures his elbow, gives up his dream of turning professional and becomes a sports photographer.' Like me, he undressed as he talked. Maybe because he'd been asleep a few minutes ago, his shoulder was warm when I brushed against it.

'Who else is in it?'

'Let's see . . . Nanako Matsushima.'

'*The* Nanako Matsushima? You've met her?'

'Yeah, I have.'

'What's she like? Is she really cute?'

'Beyond cute. So cute that it makes my stomach hurt just to sit next to her.'

Tomohiko likes long kisses. He likes to kiss so much and he doesn't like me to hold him from behind. If there really is such a thing as sexual compatibility, I think we'd pass. It's not like I'd want anyone to watch us or anything, but if someone did, I think we could be proud of our lovemaking. Lately he's had this not-so-commendable habit of timing how many seconds it takes him to put on a condom. He doesn't hand me a watch and ask me to time it, but it's obvious from how he glances at his watch right after, and grins, that he's set a new record.

We each took a shower and then we stayed in bed until he had to get back to work. His body was still slightly damp, and his hair smelled like the cheap hotel shampoo.

I was playing with his fingers and staring at our clothes, where we tossed them onto a chair, when he suddenly said, 'Oh you know, the other day when I came back late from work, there was a girl in my bed.'

'No way!'

Surprised, I sat up in bed and my head slammed into his chin.

'Ow! . . . I . . . I bit my tongue,' he said.

Tomohiko stuck out his bright red tongue and I pinched it. 'Was this girl a fan?' I asked.

'I gueth tho . . . I mean, thee didn't haf any clotheth on.'

I was still pinching his tongue as he spoke and then he started to gag.

'So what did you do?'

'Huh? I slept with her, of course.'

I could tell he was rolling his tongue around inside his mouth.

'You're kidding, right?' I glared at him.

'No, it's true. She was a fan after all.'

'She might be, but come on – she snuck into your apartment and got into your bed nude.'

'Saved me time undressing her.'

He burst out laughing and I realised he was pulling my leg. I thought he should bite his tongue one more time and tried to butt his chin again from below, but he dodged me.

In a low voice, so as not to disturb his mother, who was asleep in the next room, Tomohiko had spoken to this fan girl. She'd broken into his apartment and lay in his bed, totally nude, for some two hours, until he returned and then tried to convince her to leave. Fortunately for him the girl was pretty calm. Tomohiko told her she was too pure and needed to become more calculating, that if she likes a guy, ignoring him may be the best way to get him interested. 'I hate any kind of manoeuvring when it comes to love,' she said, but after two more hours, she took his advice and left.

Tomohiko laughed and said, 'I bet she's at home now, in front of the TV, ignoring me on purpose.' He went on, kind of proud of himself: 'I know everything about her now. The kind of food she likes, her favourite colour, her favourite film . . .'

'What's her favourite film?' I asked, grouchily.

Tomohiko tensed up a little. '*Bambi*,' he murmured. It would have been much easier to deal with if she'd liked *Misery* or something. He laughed it off, but I think he was equally put off by it.

It was getting time for us to leave the hotel, but his penis was hard again. 'I have to be back in the studio in twenty minutes,' he laughed. 'What part should we skip?'

'Just don't skip the first and last kiss,' I replied.

In the end, that's all he gave me – a first and last kiss. 'Isn't that kind of pretentious?' I kidded him.

'That's how I make a living,' he said, his nostrils flaring, which sent me into stitches.

As we took the lift down to the lobby he turned serious. 'As I explained,' he said, 'this is the way things will have to be for a while. I'm new at this work and I want to give it everything I have. So I can't make any promises now about the future. Is that okay with you?'

I told him what I'd told him last time. 'That's fine with me,' I said.

'What do you do at home all the time?' he asked, and I was about to say *Wait for you to call* but then he'd wind up saying *You have a mobile, right? So you could go out.* If I told him *Well, there's nowhere I want to go to* then that would make him feel guilty, so I lied. 'Remember how I told you the girl I live with is an illustrator? I help her out.'

'How do you pay the bills?'

'I've got some money saved up from my old job.'

'That won't last for ever.'

'When I run out, I'll get a job.'

We left the hotel and luckily there were two empty taxis parked outside. We pretended not to be together, and got in separate cabs. My driver was studying Tomohiko as he got into the taxi in front of ours and said, 'Isn't that guy on TV?'

'I'm not sure,' I said, shrugging.

'I'm certain of it. Ryo Ekura jilted him in the last episode.'

The driver finally pulled away from the kerb. Now it wasn't just girls recognising Tomohiko, but even taxi drivers! I wondered for a minute about Tomohiko's penis, which seemed harder than usual. It had me a little concerned.

I mulled over Tomohiko's words. *That won't last for ever.* Actually, I'd already used up all my savings. What *won't last for ever* is the allowance from my parents. I'm the daughter who has always begged for a little more – the one pleading with them to *trust* her *since there were things* she *wanted to do*. My mother knew I'd left home to follow an old boyfriend, so sometimes when we talked on the phone, she'd give me advice like, 'You know the more you chase a person, the more he'll run away.' But still, at the end of each month, she managed to convince my father to send me money, no doubt hoping that *if things go well she might get married*. There was no way I'd ever let on that the guy I was chasing was an up-and-coming actor. If my parents heard that, not only would the allowance stop, but the next day there'd be an emissary from my hometown on my doorstep, ready to drag me back home.

Truth be told, I don't know what I want. I meet up with Tomohiko in a hotel when he calls me like this, but I know that living together is out of the question, let alone walking down the aisle. What I dread most is being asked *Well, what do you want to do?* If someone asked me that, I'd be forced to play dead. 'There's no future in it,' Naoki warned me, about Tomohiko. 'You're wasting your time,' Mirai said. Ryosuke was the only one who said, 'I know exactly how you feel.' Sadly, though, this didn't cheer me up. A clueless college student was not the ideal confidant.

It was after eight p.m. when I got back to our apartment in Chitose Karasuyama. I was surprised to find everyone gathered in the living room. They all stared at me and then Mirai asked, pointedly, her expression stern, 'Are you the one who brought that guy here?'

'Which guy are you talking about?' I said. I was still thinking about Tomohiko, the afterglow of him welling up below my abdomen. I had no idea when I'd see him again, but was hoping that this warmth would stay with me until then.

'See, I told you Koto didn't see him,' Mirai said.

'You mean when Koto got up he was already gone?' Ryosuke asked.

'I even let him have some of my banana protein drink.'

The three of them completely ignored me, their faces serious as they leaned closer and compared notes.

'I was totally sure he was one of Ryosuke's friends from college,' Naoki said.

'Me too,' Mirai piped in, the two of them turning to Ryosuke.

'I told you I have no idea who he is,' he said. 'I never even saw him. I was sure that Mirai had got drunk and brought him home . . .'

Ryosuke looked flustered. He tried to refocus the blame on Mirai, but she and Naoki had already moved on to the question of whether the guy had stolen anything.

At some point, I decided it was time to descend back to planet earth. It was only at this point that it dawned on me that they were talking about Satoru.

'Hey, are you guys talking about Satoru?' I said and the three of them looked up at me in unison. *Come on*, their impatient faces told me, *spill it*.

'You mean Satoru, right?' I asked again, hesitantly.

They all started talking at the same time.

'*You* brought him here?'

'I get it – so he's one of Koto's *friends*.'

'You, with a young guy like that? I did *not* see that coming.'

And then I realised that they totally had the wrong idea. 'Hold on a second. I don't know him,' I told them.

'But didn't you just call him Satoru?' Mirai asked.

'You're talking about the guy who was here this morning, right?' I asked.

'That's the one.'

'But Ryosuke, isn't he one of your friends?'

I was hoping Ryosuke would come to my rescue, but he didn't. 'I told you I don't know him!' he said and looked away.

'Hang on. What's going on here?' I said. 'Who *is* that guy? I made breakfast for him, and took him to play pachinko.'

'*Pachinko?*' all three of them shouted, dumfounded.

All four of us were in an uproar after that, screaming, flinging insults back and forth about who had been the lazy idiot who came home last and forgot to lock the front door. We all kept talking about how we're way too cavalier about security and how we need to be more alert since we're living in Tokyo, and obviously, there's lots of crime. Every once in a while someone would say, 'Are you sure nothing was stolen?' and then we'd all race back to our bedrooms to check. 'Nope, nothing's missing,' someone would say; 'My piggy bank of ¥500 coins is still here,' someone else would say. And then we'd filter back into the living room. Before long we decided to sketch the guy, so that we'd have a picture to give to the police, just in case we discovered later that he had indeed robbed us. Since I was the one who had spent the most time with him – and since I pretty much felt like I was being branded as a criminal too – I described him in detail so that Mirai, a professional illustrator, could try to draw him. Once the drawing was done, Naoki looked at it and said, 'He reminds me of someone. I had the same thought when I saw him this morning,' which launched us into an extended discussion of who exactly he resembled.

Mirai went first. 'You know that guy in the film *Melody*? Doesn't he remind you of him?' Now that she mentioned it, there was some resemblance, though he wasn't the same age as the guy in the film. That much we all agreed on. So just how old is he? we wondered aloud. After batting this around for a while, we decided that Satoru, if that was really his name, was probably around seventeen, and maybe a junior in high school.

Once we'd decided his age, we rehashed the question of what he'd been doing here. Naoki and Mirai went to open a bottle of wine but Ryosuke and I grabbed it away from them.

'You'd expect him to have run away while I was in the bathroom,' Naoki said.

'Yeah, it doesn't add up. If he'd come here to rob us, why would he go back to sleep, and then wait around until Koto woke up?'

'Didn't Mirai get drunk and bring him back here?' I asked. I mean, it's not like it would be the first time.

I said this several times, but Mirai emphatically denied it. 'Now why would a seventeen-year-old guy come back with me?' she said, a little haughtily.

'Where did you go out drinking last night?' I asked her. Mirai screwed up her face, as if the events of last night were in the distant past, and she could hardly remember them. 'I had the late shift so I was there till the end,' she said, 'and I didn't leave the shop until nine. That was when the boss suggested we should go out for some dinner so we went to that Okinawan restaurant in Akasaka – you know, the one I went to with Naoki once?'

'The place where the bitter melon wasn't so bitter?'

'How can bitter melon not be bitter?'

'Come on! That's beside the point. So you went to the Okinawan restaurant, then what?'

'Let's see . . . I know we drank a lot there. Awamori. That stuff is strong! Then the boss and I went to a bar in Shimokita – the one where Ryosuke's friend works part-time.'

'Brodsky?'

'That's the place. I drank vodka there, a ton of it. And Mariné Mama showed up and said *Hey, what are you up to? Haven't heard from you in ages,* and we went straight to her bar in Shinjuku.'

'And then?'

'And then it's a little unclear . . . What I mean is, I can't exactly remember . . .'

'That must be where you met that guy and brought him home.'

'I told you that didn't happen. I just called Mama and she said *I don't think anyone like that was there. You left after two, with Laula and Silvana propping you up.'*

'Is Laula the one who looks like Mudo Oda, that chunky ex-priest who's on TV?' Ryosuke asked.

'Don't say that!' Mirai scolded. 'She's very sensitive about her looks.'

'You're telling me I went to play pachinko with a thief?' I was slowly beginning to get scared. Had I really invited him to *drop by again sometime*?

We went round and round. In the end, someone mentioned the tradition of childlike ghosts – *zashiki warashi* – appearing out of nowhere. At this point we were tired of talking about Satoru and settled on this topic for a while. Then we called it a night and everyone decided they needed a bath. And at that very instant, the doorbell rang.

At the same time, we all started to stand, then sat down again, then anxiously looked at each other.

'It can't be him again – can it?'

'No way.'

It struck me that it was lucky to have some men who lived with me. 'The door's locked, right?' someone asked, and when we realised it was, Naoki, the most courageous of the bunch, went towards it, followed by Ryosuke, and then Mirai and I, as we held on tightly to each other.

Naoki squinted out of the peephole and turned around. 'H-he's here. It's *him*,' he hissed. Ryosuke grabbed a nearby umbrella while Mirai and I, who had no weapons and nothing to grab, stood there uselessly, our hands hilariously poised in a karate-chop pose. I'm not sure why we decided this was a good idea.

'Should I leap out and grab him?' Naoki whispered and Ryosuke signalled him *Go!* And just then we heard, from the other side of the door, Satoru calling out '*Mirai*—!'

'Huh? *Me?*' Mirai took up the karate stance again.

'Is anybody there?' Satoru called out again. 'Kotomi—? Ryosuke—? Naoki—?'

Naoki was the first to make a move. He opened the door,

keeping the chain on. 'How the hell did you get in here this morning? Was the door unlocked? Or did you break in?'

From outside the door, we could hear Satoru say, hesitantly, 'What do you mean? Mirai unlocked it for me and let me in.' We all turned and glared at her. She and I had been holding on to each other, but I shook my arm free.

'It's a lie! A damn lie!' I've never seen a play staged live in a theatre, but Mirai was doing a good job of acting like she was in one. We shouldn't have been surprised, though. Mirai always got drunk and then dragged someone home with her from the bar.

At this point, Naoki had unlatched the chain and opened the door. 'Prove it! Show me some proof!' demanded Mirai, like she was still in some crummy play.

'I'm not sure how I can . . .'

Satoru was still standing at our entrance. His face lit up as he suddenly remembered. 'That's right! Someone named Laula was with us.'

'What kind of person is Laula?' Ryosuke asked.

'She's like Mudo Oda, with make-up,' Satoru replied.

'Wh-where did you meet us?' Mirai wasn't giving up.

'You remember – I was standing in a park last night and you said *I found him!* and gave me a hug. I was all *Who are you? Let go of me* and then you dragged me to some bar.'

'And Laula was with us?'

'Part of the way.'

'And I brought you back home?'

'Yeah.'

'I made you come?'

'You said if I didn't get in the taxi with you, you'd scream. Right in the middle of Yasukuni Boulevard.'

The rest of us, disgusted, filtered back to the living room. 'So who's taking a bath first?' Ryosuke asked.

'Satoru,' Naoki said, motioning to him. Satoru hesitated. 'It's okay – come on over.' I left Mirai standing at the door, with an innocent look on her face.

'She'll be practising her acting for a while, so just leave her alone,' I said to Satoru and showed him into the living room.

MIRAI SOMA (24)

3.1

If you have two weeks to spare nowadays, taking a trip around the world isn't impossible. If you're a backpacker, you can take one of those popular trips and travel by bus through Vietnam, observing the farmers toiling away, all for the purpose of *finding yourself*. I have no idea who this *real self* is that people discover. I couldn't care less if what they find is a surprisingly pathetic *self* and they slink back to Japan in defeat.

I really think I'm a snide, disagreeable sort of woman. If you ask me, as long as there are backpackers going off to observe Vietnamese farmers, that's the kind of woman I'll continue to be. Actually, they're the ones who made me like this. And while I'm at it, speaking for the simple peasants of Vietnam, I'd like to say this:

'You guys are an eyesore, hanging around our fields while we're working.'

The only way I can be a true humanitarian in Japan today is to be snide and disagreeable. That's the truth.

At any rate, if you have two weeks to spare, there are all kinds of things you can accomplish. At bookshops you see titles like *Regain your Vision in Two Weeks; Easy Two-Week Danish Egg Diet; Even You Can Knit Your Boyfriend a Jumper in Just Two Weeks; Two Weeks to Passing Pre-Level 1 of the English Proficiency Exam.* There's even one that boasts that *Through Character-Building Medical Science, 90% of Children Refusing to Attend School Will Begin Attending – In Just Two Weeks!*

So it's amazing, but in two weeks, you can do almost anything! Give me two weeks and I might turn into a famous artist, another Niki de Saint Phalle.

Two weeks . . . It's going on two weeks now since Satoru – the guy I drunkenly brought home – began living with us.

3.2

Towards morning I suddenly remembered that I needed to defrost the fridge and as I was taking care of that, Ryosuke popped up, standing right behind me. I was so into the defrosting that I didn't notice him come out from the men's bedroom. 'You're creeping me out!' I told him. 'At least say something so I know you're there!'

'You're the one creeping me out,' he snapped back, 'so I couldn't say anything.'

The guy has a point. A woman defrosting a fridge in a dark kitchen at four-thirty in the morning *is* a little spooky. But if a woman doing something like this gives you the creeps, you'll never be able to get married. Take my mum – for thirty years, without ever missing a day, she repeated the same line: *What would you like for dinner?* Talk about creepy!

Ryosuke grabbed a bottle of Volvic mineral water from the fridge and started gulping it down. He must toss and turn in bed a lot to need to rehydrate this much. He put the bottle back in the fridge and said, 'So, what are you doing?'

'Isn't it obvious?' I said, and I pulled a chunk of ice from the back of the fridge.

'Defrosting?'

'What else does it look like?' I was starting to get annoyed. Ryosuke was still wearing his PJs. He reached over and lightly massaged my shoulder. 'That's a relief,' he said.

'What do you mean?' I asked, but he just yawned and padded back to his bedroom. Imagine how worried he'd have been if I'd said something like *I hear strange voices coming from the freezer.*

Still, if you saw a woman defrosting a fridge at four-thirty in the morning, you'd probably ask what was wrong; and you probably wouldn't be relieved to hear that she's just defrosting. God, Ryosuke's so myopic! And frankly, life's too short – I have no time to deal with idiotic men. But the thing is, I thought to myself, I'm kind of fond of Ryosuke, even though he's an incredible dope.

Right then, a huge chuck of ice plopped free from inside the fridge.

In the living room, the sofa is empty, which means Satoru hasn't come back yet. He's told us that his full name is Satoru Kokubo, that he's eighteen years old, and that he *works at night.* With just this tiny bit of information about him, we let him live with us

– no questions asked – and have also opened up to him about ourselves.

Once, when Satoru was still out, the rest of us happened to be together in the living room and I asked, 'Doesn't it bother you not knowing what kind of work he does?'

'He does night work,' Naoki replied.

'But what *kind* of night work?' I asked.

'He must be a bartender or something,' Koto said.

'Where? At what kind of place?' I asked.

'It's in Shinjuku,' Ryosuke said, not looking away from Koto, who was giving herself a manicure. 'I've given him a ride there in Momoko a few times.'

Then Naoki left to go for a jog and we changed the subject. Since Satoru isn't keen on telling us whatever it is he does, I know I shouldn't be poking my nose into his business. But when I met him originally, we were in the area of Shinjuku that is notorious for being a gay district. Moreover, the park where he was hanging around is a well-known spot for male prostitutes – the really low-rent kind who steal the guy's wallet while he's in the shower. Of course, according to Mariné Mama, not every guy who hangs out there is bad news. Some are even pretty decent, she claims, and I know a few of these good guys myself, guys I'll go out drinking with. They're sweet, easy-going seventeen- or eighteen-year-olds.

Now that I've spent two weeks around Satoru, I can say that even if he is a male prostitute, I don't think he's one of the sketchy kind. Still, we've let him crash on our sofa like this, and Ryosuke, oblivious, has given him rides to 'work'. I think we should probably keep an eye on him, just in case.

It was nearly dawn – five a.m. – by the time I'd finished defrosting the fridge. I opened the window to feel the cold breeze on my cheeks, and was standing there, lingering in the afterglow of a job well done, when I heard a rustling at the front door and Satoru came in, with a bag of food from a convenience store. 'Did I wake you? Or were you already up?' he asked nonchalantly, spreading out an assortment of containers on the table: comfort food like hijiki, kinpira gobou, sesame tofu.

'So how'd you do tonight? Make any money?' I asked casually.

He shot me a quick glance, and seemed unsure whether to respond or not. Finally, as if making up his mind, he gave a thin smile and held up three fingers.

'Three people?' I asked. 'Or ¥30,000?'

With a knowing smile still on his lips, he laughed. 'That's why I showed you three fingers.'

I know this sounds self-serving, but I do think I'm a good judge of people. I don't think Satoru's going to cause me, Naoki, Koto, or Ryosuke any trouble.

3.3

Most of the drawings I do centre on male body parts. An unshaven chin, for instance, an abdomen with hair growing up to the navel, biceps, a hip bone, the sole of a foot. I take one of those body parts and make a collage out of the drawing along with pictures of rotten fruit, dirty snow and the like.

I do the illustrations on the Mac in the room Koto and I share. Sometimes I'll stay up all night working on them, and if they don't turn out well I take it out on the mouse and printer, put my head in my hands, and groan. The whole time, Koto's sleeping peacefully. You could blast the Sex Pistols' 'Anarchy in the UK', or the choral from Beethoven's Ninth – nothing will wake her up. She may be a little clueless, but she's also fearless. Take her sudden decision to catch a ride in a guy's truck to come to Tokyo – a guy she didn't even know – or her utter lack of hesitation about moving into this apartment with two men she'd never even met before. Koto has this optimistic *laxness* that you only find in a girl who's been told her whole life how cute she is, a girl who stole the heart of every boy in her class.

One night Koto and I were talking about seaweed facial packs or something. I was in bed, Koto in her futon on the floor. It was getting time to go to sleep and she asked me to turn off the light. The light switch on the wall was, for sure, closer to me than to her, but still, it was too much trouble to get out of bed.

'You know those long cords they have dangling from fluorescent lights?' I said. 'We should put one of those on this light.'

'You mean the kind with a tiny dolphin thingy on the grip?' Koto asked.

'It doesn't have to be a dolphin. But it'd be convenient, don't you think? You could turn it off without getting out of bed.'

Usually Koto would just say *Sounds good* and leave it at that, but this time, for once, she grumbled about it. 'Yeah,' she went on, 'but things that are convenient are generally pretty crummy.'

If I had to give one reason why Koto and I could live together in this tiny room without ever fighting, that's the line I'd list.

One other time, I can't remember when exactly, Koto said, 'You know, living here I feel like I'm in an Internet chat room.' At the time, I just ignored her, but later, when I thought about it some more, I saw she had a point. I get that chat room kind of feeling when I'm in the living room, because there's always someone present: Koto and Ryosuke watching TV, Ryosuke and Naoki arm-wrestling on occasion. Sometimes, of course, I'm the only one there and I plonk down on the sofa. But once I sit down, somebody invariably wanders in.

But the basic right everyone has in a chat room is to be anonymous, which of course we are not. We not only know each other's names, but even each other's parents' names. The magical genie of anonymity isn't necessarily what you think . . . Most people think that anonymity allows us to reveal our true natures, but I doubt it. If I were to do something anonymously I don't think I'd reveal my true self. Instead, I'd play the impostor, exaggerating one thing after another. Nowadays *being yourself* is seen as a virtue. The only image I get, though, of people who are *being themselves* is of someone who is negligent and sloppy.

Maybe this was exactly what Koto was trying to say. The only way to live here is to play the role of the perfect self that fits into this place. And this isn't a serious performance. If a serious role is what you're after you'd best go to the Bungakuza theatre, or hang out with the famous theatre troupe En.

Maybe I'm not being clear. But here's what I mean:

The *me* who lives here is most definitely the *Apartment Me* I created, and by that I mean she's someone who just doesn't do serious. So the real me doesn't actually exist here, in this apartment. The me who gets along well with the other residents (Ryosuke, Koto, Naoki, and Satoru) is *Apartment Me* . . . But maybe they've also created their own *Apartment Selves*, too. Which would mean that they, too, don't actually exist in this apartment. Conclusion? No one is in this apartment. If this is a deserted apartment, then I don't have to worry about a thing. No need to go to the trouble of creating an *Apartment Me*. I can be more bold, with no constraints . . . No, that's not right. For me to live like that – boldly, with no constraints – this place has to be deserted. And for that to happen, we all need to have our own *Apartment Selves*. We are the only ones who can create these *Apartment Selves*, which means that all of us must actually be here – Ryosuke, who tosses and turns all night; Koto, who stays glued to the TV; Naoki with his morning protein drinks; Satoru, who, although he's so young, eats old-fashioned dishes like hijiki – and me – all packed into this stifling, overcrowded space. It's actually a fully occupied space, yet there's no one here. Yet even though none of us are really here, it's still fully occupied. Ugh. It makes my head spin! I wish I could say I get it, but I don't.

3.4

I was working the late shift, so I slept in and got up just before noon. I took a shower, stuffed a leftover rice ball in my mouth, and was heading towards the door and out to work when I nearly bumped into Koto crouched down amidst the tangle of shoes, peering out through the letterbox in the front door.

'What're you doing?' I asked. She whipped around and put her index finger to her lips.

'Wh-what is it? Is somebody there?'

'Shh!' Koto said and again stuck her face close to the letterbox. Jostling her aside with my hips, I crouched down beside her and peered out through the slot. In the hallway outside, Ryosuke and the man from apartment 402 were standing there, talking.

'What's Ryosuke up to?' I whispered to Koto.

'I made him go undercover,' Koto replied. She made a face that reminded me of the actress Nagisa Katahira on the show *Tuesday Suspense*.

'What do you mean, undercover?'

'Ryosuke's going inside 402 as a client.'

Koto nudged me aside and I fell on my bum, landing on Naoki's loafers.

'Well, until the fourth of next month, then,' I could hear Ryosuke say on the other side of the door. The man from 402 returned to his apartment. Koto stood up, slowly opened the door, and let Ryosuke in. He, too, reminded me of a rookie detective from a suspense drama.

'How'd it go?' she asked.

'Perfect.'

'So he admitted what's going on?'

'At first I tried to trick him, saying I knew what was going on, but he just said *What are you talking about?* and pretended not to know. When I told him things could get complicated if the management company finds out what's going on, he said, "Guess I have no choice then . . . But I don't usually take on young men as clients. And we're only open three days before and after a full moon; and three days before and after a new moon. This month we're already booked. I guess we could do the fourth of next month." So I made an appointment for that day. Then we'll find out what's really going on.'

'I suppose. But still . . .'

'What?'

'Since he's already admitted what's going on, is there still a need to go undercover?'

'You mean I shouldn't go?'

I was still sitting on my backside, listening, when Ryosuke finally noticed me. 'What're you doing there?' he said, helping to pull me to my feet.

'You guys are nuts, you know that?' I said.

They completely ignored me and headed to the living room. Their dialogue went on: 'How much did he say it would be?' 'Usually it's ¥30,000, but he said since we're neighbours he'd make it ¥20,000.' 'Wow! That much?'

I slipped on my shoes and called out a goodbye. But instead of the usual farewell their loud voices continued: 'That's expensive!' 'No, it's cheap!'

I don't know if the two of them were really serious, but I couldn't care less if the man next door ran a brothel, a video pirating operation, or whatever. If he ran his washing machine in the middle of the night, or threw all his recyclables into the regular rubbish – now *then* I'd wouldn't let him get away with it.

3.5

The boutique where I work mainly sells imported goods: batiks, ikat, and ornaments and accessories from India and Bali. It's a small chain, with two stores in Harajuku, one each in Kawasaki and Honmoku. I manage the second store in Harajuku.

Four years ago, when Shinji, the owner, interviewed me at a

coffee shop in Omotesando, he went on for a good hour and a half about all the troubles he'd had in life, like he was ecstatic to finally have someone to talk to. After college he'd gone to work for an apparel company but it went bankrupt, so he made a fresh start, using money he borrowed from his parents to start a company that imported Mexican leather goods. His business partner wound up taking off with the money he'd invested. The man had been his friend since high school and he always thought they'd be friends for ever. Shinji went all the way to far-off Asahikawa looking for his friend, and, one day, tired from walking the streets, he went into a ramen shop. As he slurped up the hot noodles, tears of frustration rolled down his cheeks . . . When he got to this point in his story I couldn't help but cry in sympathy. 'Don't cry,' he told me, welling up himself. 'But look how well things worked out,' I said, the tears coming again. 'You've got a wonderful business going now.'

I doubt anybody else in the coffee shop would have ever guessed this was a job interview.

Shinji is partly to blame for how, night after night, I make the rounds of bars. He's the one who first took me to the Blue Note in Aoyama, to expensive clubs in Ginza, to the Shinjuku Golden Gai bar area, the gay district, even to the exclusive Gora Kadan spa in Hakone. He was the one who showed me, when I was barely twenty and just a girl from the sticks, how to party. People misunderstood our relationship – they were sure we were sleeping together – but honestly, nothing like that ever happened. If he had tried something, I would have turned him down flat, and if he'd been nasty because of it, I would have quit my job right then and there.

I know this is kind of a stale metaphor, but the first time

Shinji took me to a bar in Shinjuku 2-chome it was startling, like I was catching my first glimpse of heaven. Now that I think of it, the first place we went to was Mariné Mama's bar. The counter and booths were packed with swarms of young men, like fruit at the peak of ripeness. Not a single one looked in my direction. That sense of freedom was as if, right now, in my shop, I were completely naked and the male customers in the store ignored me and instead went on and on about how one of their colleagues has a bottle of Givenchy Ultramarine cologne in his house. If Koto had been there she might have said, warily, 'This isn't good – you're the only woman in the whole place,' but for me, far from being wary at all, I felt liberated. It was a strange sort of paradise where even the worst villain was welcome to come on in.

On the application form to enter this accessible heaven, there's a part that asks for your gender. There's a part that says *Male* and *Female,* and beside that, there's a box you can check that simply says *Person.*

3.6

Two or three days ago Naoki and I went to eat yakiniku grilled meat at a place near the station. He had a couple of days off in a row, unusual for him. As he stirred up the raw egg on top of his yukke, he said, 'When I see a girl on the train listening to a Walkman or something, it gets me excited.'

'How come?' I asked.

'I don't know . . . it might be a kind of fetish, but when I stand behind a woman who's completely cut off from sounds around her, I feel like slowly licking her from behind, from her ear down to her neck.' He looked totally serious as he confessed this.

'Then the listening corner at Tower Records or the Virgin store would be like your own personal harem.'

I was joking, of course, but as he wrapped his kalbe up in a lettuce leaf, he said, 'Wow – you're right!' like he was really impressed by the idea.

The apartment we're living in now was originally rented by Naoki and Misaki. They were a couple, of course, and though they must have had a honeymoon period, soon after I moved in they started sleeping in separate bedrooms. Shinji had introduced us and Misaki and I got to be good drinking buddies.

One night we were at Mariné Mama's and I was complaining how the lease on my place was up for renewal but since I'd caused a car accident I was totally broke.

Mama said, 'Come over to my place. I have an extra room.'

'You can stay with us,' Misaki said. 'We have room.'

Mama has a vicious cat who has it in for me. In Misaki's place there's just gentle Naoki, who likes to drink as much as me. Misaki had brought Naoki a few times to Mama's, so I'd met him already.

I remember once when he was at the bar and Mama asked him, 'If you had to do it with a man, who would you pick?' and Naoki replied, 'If I really had to do it, I think I'd like to sleep with an intellectual, like Roland Barthes or Michel Foucault.' Most heterosexual men, when Mama asks them this, give the names of fighters.

'Sounds like you could expect a sermon in bed,' Mama said, laughing.

'You prefer the body over the intellect, I see,' Naoki said, himself laughing.

'That's right. I'm always sleeping with meat, so my cholesterol goes up,' she replied.

'From what I hear, though, you always choose fresh meat,' I cut in.

'True. But fresh meat is always so expensive,' Mama laughed.

'Come on, you know you're raking in the money. Word on the street is you buy it not by the ounce but by the pound.' Naoki had only had a couple of drinks at this point.

Actually I wasn't remembering this conversation when I made the decision. Instead I put the vicious cat on one side of the scales, and mild-mannered, fashionable Naoki on the other, and turned to Misaki, not Mama, and said, in a coaxing tone, 'I'll take you up on your offer. Is it okay if I move in next month?'

I'd been expecting things not to work out so well, but the communal life the three of us had – Misaki, a secretary at a huge cosmetics company; Naoki, who works at an independent film distributor; and me, an illustrator who managed an import boutique – turned out to be much better than I ever imagined. It's like a camera on a tripod – three legs and it stands up, two legs and it falls over.

In the beginning Misaki and Naoki used what is now the girls' room and I had what is now the guys' room to myself. Then Misaki complained that Naoki talked in his sleep and it bothered her, so she made him stay by himself in the guys' room and I moved into the girls' room with her. About half a year after the three of us had started living together, Naoki brought Ryosuke to live with us – he was a younger classmate of someone who was a younger classmate of Naoki's at college. Misaki and I should have asked Naoki why he wanted Ryosuke to move in, but instead all we asked was, pointlessly, 'What? A college student?' We felt left out of the decision, but we told him it was okay. Now that I think about it, Misaki must have already been considering breaking up with Naoki at this point.

It wasn't long after this that Misaki starting going out with a middle-aged bachelor from her company and spending most of her time at his place. By the time she was staying most of every week there, I asked Naoki about it.

'Are you okay with this?' I asked him.

And he said, 'Sure. How about you?'

'What do you mean?'

'If Misaki leaves here then you'll be one woman with two men.'

'That's why I want you to stop counting that way.'

'How should I count?'

'Three people is fine. Three *people*.'

And Misaki really did leave. Naoki borrowed a truck for her move and Ryosuke and I helped out. But Misaki still continues to drop by. And when she feels like it, she stays over a few days, sleeping on the sofa in the living room. Even Ryosuke wonders what's going on. 'What a second,' he'll say, 'didn't Misaki and Naoki break up?' It's hard to explain their relationship now. I guess a relationship that's easy to explain isn't much of one to begin with, but still I think it's pretty odd how happy Naoki is when Misaki stops by. And Misaki's pretty odd too. I mean, she's living with another guy, yet she comes to her old boyfriend's place, says, 'This is where I can breathe easy,' and seems totally relaxed.

3.7

I had a terrible hangover and, clutching a bottle of Volvic, I'd collapsed on the sofa. There was a memo on the table: *Gone to the hair salon*, Koto had written, and on the back *I've got nothing else to do so I went with her. Satoru.*

It was just a little after noon when the doorbell rang. I dragged myself to the entrance and when I opened the heavy front door, there stood two uniformed cops.

It was the middle of the day but my hair was all over the place, I was dressed in rumpled pyjamas, and my face was pale. The two cops took one look at me and must have thought I was ill. They quickly explained the reason for their visit, bowed, and left. 'We hope you feel better,' they told me.

It seems that recently in our neighbourhood two women on their way home had been attacked from behind by a man and bashed in the face. The attacks had taken place one after the other. Luckily the first woman wasn't injured badly, but the woman who'd been assaulted the other day had a broken nose. Both attacks had taken place on the opposite side of the station, the police said, but still they cautioned me to be careful if I was walking alone at night, and to have a man go with me, if possible.

I went back to the sofa and told myself I'd have to tell Koto to be careful, too. Ah! That's right! I told myself, this time out loud. When the policemen had asked if I lived alone I'd told them I lived with a friend. 'So there're two women living here?' they asked, and I said, 'No, two men and two women. Four people in all.'

I picked up the memo on the table again and reread the back, written in Satoru's childish writing: *I've got nothing else to do so I went with her.*

3.8

I knew I wasn't going to sell anything, but still I went to Inokashira Park, next to the pond, to try to sell some of my illustrations. I dragged Koto along with me. I laid out a black cloth on the ground and spread out my latest illustrations (ones with the theme of men's navels) and was waiting for potential customers to stop by when an elderly man, a gentlemanly type with salt-and-pepper hair, came up and painstakingly examined each and every drawing. Whenever I have Koto sit next to me it's amazing how many men stop by. They pretend to look at the drawings as they steal glances at her, but this man was different. He didn't give her a single glance and concentrated instead on my illustrations.

'Are there any in particular you like?' I asked. Normally I just let people browse, but the man was so totally intent on my work that I couldn't help but speak up. He didn't even raise his head at this, and continued scanning the drawings.

In the end the man left without saying anything.

'What was that all about?' Koto asked.

'Guess he didn't like them,' I said, grouchily.

It was then that I realised how much I was dying to be discovered. I'd been hoping, as I sat there on the cold stone pavement of the park, that the man might turn out to be an art dealer from Ginza or Aoyama, or a curator who lived in New York who was the first person to recognise my genius. It's almost embarrassing how much I was hoping this was true.

I've never yet sold a drawing at a park or on the pavement. I've had drunk old guys about to buy one, but I always politely turn them down. In times like those I understand how I've still got a long way to go as an artist. Someday, though, I'd like to draw the kind of works that drunks would not only be unable to buy, but wouldn't even be able to look at.

It was about an hour later when that elderly man reappeared. Again he came up and, without a word, carefully looked through each drawing. After a while he looked up and asked, 'Are these navels?'

'Y-yes, they are,' I replied, flustered.

'Ah – so they're navels. I guess they are, now that you mention it.'

After he said this, the man went away again.

'So *they're navels*, he says,' Koto laughed and I laughed with her.

Is there some other way – other than trying to laugh it off – to deal with frustration?

3·9

Last night Ryosuke called a group meeting and we all assembled in the living room. Naoki and I were of course a little buzzed, while Koto, who's crazy about the video game *Biohazard 2*, was playing it with Satoru, before he went to work. All of us sat there listening to Ryosuke, who stood in front of us, legs set wide apart.

Ryosuke told us that this weekend he'd invited the girlfriend of his older college friend, Umezaki – the one who'd given him the washing machine – for dinner and he wanted us all to clear our schedules since he'd really like us to join them.

Sounds good, we agreed and were heading back to our own rooms when Ryosuke stopped us. 'Actually I have another favour I need to ask you,' he said.

'What else?' I asked, sort of irritated.

'I hope you're not going to ask us to help you steal Umezaki's girlfriend from him,' Naoki said.

'Is there something you want us to say to her?' Koto went on.

'Like bring up a selling point, tell her how good you are at something?' Satoru laughed.

Ryosuke visibly flinched, so we knew they'd hit the mark.

'So what do you want us to say to her?' I laughed, and Koto said, '*He doesn't look like much, but he's actually very manly.* Something like that?'

'Any girl who'd fall for that isn't worth much,' Satoru said, and everyone nodded deeply in agreement. For eighteen, he was a surprisingly good judge of women.

'If there's something you want us to say, write it down,' Naoki said and was heading to his room.

'Actually, I do have something,' Ryosuke said, and pulled out some sheets of paper with writing on it.

He'd already prepared copies of a script for us to use at dinner, five whole pages of paper. The script began with Ryosuke introducing his friend's girlfriend, Kiwako, to all of us. The names of each speaker were indicated before the lines on the script.

'The heck with this,' Naoki and I said, and went back to our rooms, but it was almost scary how much Koto and Satoru, who had way too much time on their hands, were suddenly into it.

They each played two different parts, and with Ryosuke instructing them in no uncertain terms – *No, that's too obvious! – Do that part again!* – they practised until late into the night.

I tried to concentrate on drawing in my room, doing my best not to be bothered by the school play going on in the living room, but Koto's voice as she repeated one line – 'Ryosuke is a chameleon – when he likes someone, he loves whatever they like most' – stuck with me for some reason and I couldn't get any work done at all. *Person he likes* must mean his friend Umezaki. When I thought of Kiwako sitting there, forced to eat dinner while lines like that flew back and forth, I couldn't help but feel sorry for the poor girl.

I finally was focused on my drawing for a while when I heard Satoru dramatically call out a line, like he was on stage at the Takarazuka Review: 'Sometimes this is what I think. I want to be the kind of person who lives life on his own terms!' They must have woken up Naoki, who shouted out: 'Shut up! You think that way, that's why you're so damned noisy!' I remembered that Naoki had to get up the next morning to go to Narita Airport to meet a film director coming from France.

As I imagined Naoki tossing and turning, unable to sleep, I lined up on my desk the reference photos of Ryosuke and Satoru's backs that I'd taken the other day.

3.10

Until last year this transvestite named Ken – a pretty heroic name, *ken* the character for sword – worked at Mariné Mama's. He and

I were great friends, so much so that when I was still living by myself in Yutenji, before I moved in here, and Ken had been dumped by his married boyfriend, I let him stay at my place for a while.

Last night was the third anniversary of Ken's death.

Ken got drunk one day, ran out of the bar and was hit by a taxi and died. As often happened with him, he'd fallen for a married man, been cruelly dumped and was pretty upset. Mama and her customers heard a dull *thud*, raced outside and found, just beyond the taxi, Ken lying in the middle of the road, dressed, as usual, in women's clothing. With stifled shrieks everyone rushed over, and Ken opened his eyes once, smiled, said, 'I'm okay, I'm okay,' and lost consciousness. 'One of his red high heels was lying by an electric pole,' Mama recalled.

Naturally I attended the funeral, which took place in his hometown of Sendai. Mama and his other friends from the bar came along, but they asked me to attend the funeral alone. 'Ken told his family he was working in advertising,' they said and, worried about what the other mourners might think, they just stood at a distance across the street from the funeral home and watched as his coffin was being carried out.

While I was waiting for Ken to be cremated, I went into the lobby of the building and was having a smoke when his older sister called out to me. I was the only woman who'd come all the way from Tokyo for the funeral and was wondering how I should introduce myself when she said, 'I know all about him.

'Father doesn't know a thing,' she continued, 'but Mum and I figured out what kind of job he was doing . . . Those were all his friends outside the funeral parlour, weren't they? I was thinking I should go over and say hello . . . A little while ago Mum said this: "Ken must have been a very happy person to have so many friends".'

I didn't say anything, and was thinking that Mariné Mama should be hearing this.

It was about six months after Ken's funeral when I got a call from his sister, asking me to take her to the bar where he'd worked. It turned out she and her mother were already in Tokyo. I contacted Mama right away.

Ken's sister and mother were pretty shocked when they saw the photo of him on the wall of the bar dressed up as a nurse, but both of them could drink a lot, and as we drained a whole bottle of Ken's favourite whisky, Four Roses Black Label, the atmosphere started to mellow out.

'That girl always fell for married men and then got dumped,' Mama said, pulling no punches. 'He never learned. I think his hippocampus must have been damaged.'

'It must run in the family, then,' his mother slurred. 'I stole his father away from another woman when I married him.'

We reminisced about Ken until the wee hours of the morning, and by the time his mother and sister had to go back to Sendai they were big fans of Mama's bar.

Last night, at the third anniversary memorial service at the bar, his mother and sister were there, of course. It was hard to believe how nervous they'd been the first time I'd taken them there, 'cause this time his mother was behind the bar, mixing drinks for the customers with Mama, while his sister ran through a whole rendition of the song Ken and I used to perform together – Wink's 'Boys Don't Cry' – complete with all the dance steps.

The night I came back from Ken's funeral I was so

overcome with grief I didn't know what to do, so I asked Ryosuke, who'd just started living with us, to take me for a drive in Momoko.

I didn't tell Ryosuke that a close friend had just died. I just asked him to drive me around all night – I didn't care that we had to stop every nine kilometres. I sat there sobbing in the passenger seat but Ryosuke didn't ask me anything, he silently kept on driving. At one point, though, when we stopped at a petrol station in Harumi to fill up, he said, jokingly, 'Heavy drinkers do seem to cry differently.' I'm grateful to Ryosuke for that night. I'm happy he could be by my side.

Come to think of it, two months ago Ryosuke surprised me by asking me to go with him on a drive, and we drove all around until the next morning. 'Is anything the matter?' I asked him several times, but he just said, 'Not really,' and kept his eyes on the road. Instead, he asked, 'Hey, do you know when Disney Sea is going to open?' 'Are you going to go?' I asked and he said, 'No, a friend of mine from junior high said he's coming.' I wasn't interested, and said I didn't know. 'Really?' Ryosuke said, and said no more.

3.11

I bought a bento at Karasu Bento, came back home and found Koto and Satoru huddled in the living room, deep in the midst of a discussion about what they should submit for the contest to name the shopping area in front of the station. The first prize was ¥1,000,000.

'Since the area's called Chitose Karasuyama – with the word "crow" in there, *karasu* – how about "Caw Caw Road"?'

'I bet a hundred other people have come up with that one.'

Koto and Satoru are always together during the day and have grown close.

I suddenly realised I hadn't had a call from my mother the whole week. Nothing could be better, but still, not hearing from her always worries me. I think it was about ten days ago when she called last. I was just back from work and Koto had said, 'You had a call from your mother.'

'What'd she say?' I asked.

'Nothing really, but I think she was drunk. She was kind of laughing uproariously, sounded kind of happy,' Koto replied, unfazed.

My mum calls me, drunk in the middle of the day, laughing uproariously, and Koto says she's in a good mood.

Sometimes I wish it was all a joke – all the scenes I can't help remembering, of Dad slamming the door and Mum crouching in fear, of Mum reeking of alcohol and Dad grabbing her by the arm, or me running upstairs, crying in my room. Sometimes I wish I could just add some silly background music to it all, like the entrance music when the comedian Ken Shimura plays his moronic stock samurai character on TV.

I think it was back in high school. One day I was going to the kitchen to get some juice when I overheard my parents in the next room. Dad was apparently pinning Mum down against her will, and I heard him growl out in a low voice, 'That's what I married you for, right?'

3.12

I had the day off and when I woke up in the morning I was feeling – for the first time in I don't know how long – so refreshed I decided to put all my winter clothes away. Koto usually does a great job of vacuuming and our room and the living room are so clean you could eat off the floor.

I opened the wardrobe and was stuffing a thick coat and jumper into a cardboard box when I ran across an old plastic bag from a Lawson's convenience store. I knew without opening it what was inside – a 120-minute Sony video tape tossed in like so much rubbish.

The video tape had all the rape scenes from films that I knew recorded on it. Like the last scene in the film *Cinema Paradiso*, where the main character watched a film of all these movie kiss scenes spliced together, this tape contained a dozen or so rape scenes. Like the scene in *The Accused*, where Jodi Foster is raped on top of a pinball machine. The scene in *A Clockwork Orange* where a girl is raped with 'Singing in the Rain' playing in the background. Girls in *Last Exit to Brooklyn*, *Blue Velvet*, *Thelma and Louise* all crying for the men to *stop it!* In *Straw Dogs* and *Class of 1984*, the men rape women as the heroes in a revenge drama. Greenaway's *The Baby of Mâcon*, Bergman's *The Virgin Spring*. One woman after another getting raped, enough to make you want to puke. No other scenes at all. Just rape scenes going on and on. Based on these scenes you don't get any idea of the women's backgrounds, like where they live, what kind of work they do, what kind of flowers they like, what dreams they have, whether they're married, or have kids. No info on that at all. All you see are women struggling to get away from men.

Ever since I started living with Naoki and Misaki in this apartment I haven't watched the tape. When I used to live alone in Yutenji sometimes, when I couldn't sleep, I'd play it.

For some strange reason, whenever I watched these spliced-together rape scenes it calmed me down. My feelings of how cruel, miserable, and pitiful it all was gradually faded away, and the expressions of the faces of the rape victims ended up looking like people having a great time at a festival. The timidity I'd had, the sort of vague dread and insomnia, were steadily numbed. Watching these women – men pressing their hands on their mouths, forcing their arms and legs down, prying open their thighs, the women struggling without being able to scream – I came to enjoy it, as if they were dancing in time to music.

3.13

Naoki had come home slightly tipsy, and Ryosuke was clinging to him, apparently begging him to lend him ¥30,000. 'I promise I'll pay you back when I get paid for my part-time job at the end of the month,' Ryosuke pleaded. Koto and I were on the sofa eating ice cream, enjoying this little scene played out before us.

'What're you going to use it for?' Naoki asked.

We could hear them in their room now, where it seemed like Naoki was taking off his suit and Ryosuke was hanging it up for him. 'So if you could just see your way to lending it to me,' Ryosuke said, continuing to pester him.

'I'll lend it to you if you'll tell me what you're going to use it for.' Naoki had now stripped down to his underwear. He strode out into the living room with Ryosuke trotting along behind him, his bath towel in hand.

'If I tell you, will you really lend it to me?'

'Sure. As long as it's not for something weird.'

'It isn't. I need it for a date.'

'A date? With Kiwako?'

'Of course. Who else?'

Seated next to me, licking her green tea ice cream, Koto said, 'Ryosuke already asked Satoru.' She sounded a bit disgusted by it.

'You begged an eighteen-year-old for money?' I burst out. 'Don't you have any pride?'

'Yeah, but he's loaded.'

'He's right,' Koto said, nodding deeply. 'When I went to play pachinko with him he pulled out ¥10,000 bills from his pocket one after another.'

I wondered whether male prostitutes these days were really doing that well, but all I said was 'Hmmmm' and let it go. Naoki grabbed the bath towel out of Ryosuke's hands, said, 'Okay. I'll give it to you,' and went into the bath. Ryosuke stood there in front of the closed bathroom door and gave a triumphant fist pump.

'Where're you going to go with ¥30,000?' I asked.

'It's a secret,' Ryosuke replied slyly, and retreated back into the guys' room.

'It's a kind of talent,' Koto murmured beside me.

'What is?' I asked.

'How he can coax people to do things.'

Ryosuke really does have that ability. The fact that he doesn't realise it makes you think that all the more, but sometimes you just can't help stepping in to take care of him, when he acts so helpless it makes you mad. I imagine that talent alone – the ability to get people to do what he wants – should be enough to get him through life.

That's right – the other day Ryosuke finally brought Kiwako, whom we'd heard so much about, back to the apartment. When I got back from work Koto and Satoru were already in the midst of the stupid little play Ryosuke had scripted, repeating their lines like a pair of mynah birds. Kiwako had long since seen through their act, and when I came into the living room she sidled up to me and said, 'They've got to stop reading those lines. I can't take it.'

Before I actually met her, I was sure that Kiwako, who was clearly cheating on her boyfriend with a younger guy, must be a terrible sort of woman. But actually she turned out to be quite nice. I could understand how Ryosuke would fall for her, and I even found myself hoping that she would take Ryosuke, who acts pretty spoiled, and turn him into a stand-up guy. Not that the kind of man I see as decent is the type who other people would call decent.

That evening, after we had a lively dinner, Ryosuke went to the car park to get Momoko – a good twenty-minute walk – and while he was gone Kiwako and I were standing outside our building, talking.

We were talking about her younger brother she was living with – he wanted to be a musician – when she suddenly asked, 'Oh – I wanted to ask you this, but is Ryosuke kind of . . . fragile? Like, has he ever suddenly burst into tears?'

'Burst into tears?'

'Um. Has he?'

'Well, I've never seen him . . . Did he do that with you?'

'Not really.'

She clammed up and right then Ryosuke pulled up alongside us in Momoko. 'Sorry to keep you waiting!' he called out, and seeing that happy-go-lucky face I couldn't picture him as ever fragile enough to burst into tears.

3.14

I was bar hopping in Shinjuku with Laula, amongst the nightclubs and gay bars – Laula had just declared that her dream was to be the matron of a dorm for a high school baseball team – when we saw Satoru and a young colleague of his, seated on a park bench, clearly not having much luck attracting customers.

Thinking I'd surprise him, we scrambled over the park fence and came up behind them, and as we did we heard Satoru speaking in a very heated voice. Laula was about to spring out of the bushes but I held her back and we eavesdropped on their conversation for a while.

'So he tied up my arms and legs, and I was on the floor like a sushi roll, when three more guys came out, all built like pro wrestlers like him. They must have been hiding in the next room.'

'Are you serious? And all of them did you?'

'Not just that, they kicked me and beat me, and the next morning I had to go to the hospital.'

'Did they pay you?'

'Yeah, but I had blood coming out of my arse for a week, and my face was so bruised nobody else would buy me for a while. It was awful.'

'We're bound to get killed someday.'

'Either that or not be marketable any more. One or the other.'

Laula was fighting off the mosquitoes in the bushes, and she loudly slapped at one. Satoru and his friend instinctively turned at the sound and started to run away. 'It's not the police,' I called out to them. 'It's me!'

After that I took Satoru and the other boy, who called himself Makoto, out drinking. However many bars later we got to be friends with a man, a well-off manufacturer of sweets from Kobe, and rented out the bar for the rest of the night so we could have our own private karaoke party. As Satoru hooted at the older customers to get lost, and started a strip show on top of the counter, I began belting out my favourite golden oldie, Naoko Kawai's 'Smile for Me'.

Satoru and his friend must have been on something before we hooked up with them, since they were totally high. Before I knew what was going on they'd both stripped naked, raced out of the bar, and made a human pyramid on the street outside.

I can't remember how late we stayed. All I recall is Satoru carrying me on his back to the next bar.

I came to in a taxi. Satoru was beside me and when I asked where we were he said, 'We just got in a taxi. We're outside Isetan department store.'

I started acting up again but he restrained me.

'It's warm tonight so why don't I take you to this nice place I know.'

We were getting on Kyukoshu Kaido Boulevard when he said this.

'I hope they have something to drink at this *nice place?*' I asked, but he didn't answer.

I'm in my seventh year in Tokyo but this was the first time I'd ever set foot in Hibiya Park. Like Satoru said, it was a peaceful spring night, and once inside the park grounds you could still feel on your skin the strong odour of warm grass from the daytime. We cut through a square surrounded by dark trees and came to a quiet pond and a fountain reflecting the moon. We looked at our reflections on the surface of the water. Following Satoru's lead, I dipped my finger in the water and watched the ripples shake, ever so slightly, the image of the moon.

Where he led me was an outdoor amphitheatre.

'Is this it?' I asked.

'Right. Inside there,' pointing to the top of a fence.

'We're climbing over it?'

'Yep.'

With Satoru pushing my bum from behind, I scrambled over the fence.

A series of benches radiated out from a round stage. Since this was an outdoor concert venue, there was no roof, just the purple urban sky overhead. The place could easily hold five hundred people. I stood there alone for a while.

Satoru finally climbed over the fence and asked, 'So, do you like it?'

'Like you ever had any doubt,' I grinned back.

As he led me by the hand past the seats towards the stage, Satoru said, 'I've spent the night here sometimes.'

'Isn't it cold in the winter?'

'I don't stay in the winter. I'd freeze to death.'

'Before you came to our place, where did you sleep?'

'Different places. At saunas, at friends'.'

'In clients' apartments?'

'Yeah.'

I lay down on top of the stage. It felt like I hadn't looked straight up at the night sky for ages. Satoru sat down next to me and clutched his knees. He pulled out an assortment of things from his jeans pocket and lined them up next to him. A crumpled ¥10,000 bill, a piece of already-chewed gum in a silver wrapper, an army knife, a wire, a condom. In a crushed box of Mild Seven cigarettes there were a couple of joints mixed in. I had him light one up for me and took a hit as I gazed up at the sky.

'Do you smoke in our apartment?' I asked him. The purplish smoke lazily rose into the night sky.

'No, I don't. I did it once and Naoki yelled at me, told me to go smoke on the balcony.'

'Makes sense. He doesn't even drink coffee – he says it's healthier not to.'

For a while we gazed up at the sky. 'At times like this,' Satoru muttered, 'people tend to talk about childhood memories.'

'Is that what you want to do?' I teased him. I was definitely not at my most charming.

'Not particularly.'

'Why not? This is the perfect moment, so you should go ahead.' I poked him on the shoulder.

'I don't mind,' he said, laughing. 'I mean it's all made up anyway.'

The thought suddenly hit me: there are types of lies where you announce them ahead of time.

3.15

For the first time in a long while, I left work without having a drop to drink. When I got home I could hear Ryosuke and Satoru's voices from the guys' room. Koto was apparently out on a date with Tomohiko, their first in quite a few weeks. The living-room table was full of her make-up clutter. Naoki was still at work. I gargled in the bathroom and plonked myself down in the living room, unoccupied for once, picked up the remote from the floor and switched on the TV. I was eating a Karasu bento, my second in two days, when the TV reception started to go crazy. I stood up, disposable chopsticks clamped in my mouth, and smacked the right side of the TV three times: once hard, then hard again, and then softly, just like Koto had taught me. Usually when the TV set was zapping you could still hear the audio, but recently there was static in the audio, too. I smacked it again – hard, hard, then soft. The picture wavered a lot, then settled back as before, like nothing had happened. And then I heard Ryosuke's voice from his room.

'It's kind of embarrassing to say this, but I really respect my dad.'

Ryosuke respecting his father? That was news to me. I'd never heard him say this before.

'Did I ever tell you this?' he went on. 'My father runs a sushi shop. Not that that's relevant, but anyway when my dad was young it seems he ran around a lot. Maybe this is strange coming from his son, but he was sort of a leader, and took good care of the people he hung out with. So even now the guys in his crew when he was young still follow him, call him *Chief*. When I see that side of him, it's like, I don't know – I don't think someone like me can ever be better than him as a person, and when I'm with him I feel like I sort of shrink back. I'm always wondering how I should respond to him to make him happy, what I can do to win his approval. That's all I can think of when I'm with him, even now.'

I don't know if Satoru was seriously listening to Ryosuke or not, but from the living room I couldn't hear his voice at all.

'You know, it's like unconsciously the reason I came all the way to Tokyo was so I could outdo my dad at something. But here I am, and there's not a single person who wants to imitate me, and I seriously doubt I've become the type of person anybody would feel that way about.'

As I listened to Ryosuke's earnest confession, I tried to keep from bursting out laughing. Here was a guy who had no qualms about hitting up a younger guy for money; and now he was desperately hoping to be admired. It was laughable.

'You know, one time – just once, mind you – there was a guy I'm pretty sure depended on me. He was a classmate of mine in junior high. His name was Shinya. He really counted on me. At least I'm pretty sure that's what was going on . . .'

'So what happened?' Satoru asked. 'When this Shinya guy was depending on you so much?'

'Huh? Well . . .' Ryosuke began and then fell quiet.

Silence for a while and then I heard Satoru's voice, trying to stifle his laughter: 'So you couldn't be counted on after all?'

'Knock it off! . . . What I think is, when people count on someone, when they're seriously counting on them, the person they're counting on doesn't realise it. I mean – they might notice it, but they don't understand how seriously, how desperately, the other person's depending on them.'

I'd finished my bento and tossed it in the bin. I felt like taking a shower, so I went to the girls' room to get some clean underwear. *When people count on someone, the person they're counting on doesn't realise it.* For some reason, I couldn't shake Ryosuke's words.

I was on my way to the bathroom, clean underwear in hand, when this time I heard Satoru's voice. I stopped outside the guys' bedroom and listened in.

'I was an only child and my mum raised me all by herself,' Satoru was saying. 'I always wanted someone like an older brother, someone I could talk to, and get advice from. I wouldn't mind if we fought most of the time, and I couldn't stand the sight of him. That'd be okay with me. When something came up, it would have been great to have someone I could talk to, even if he lived far away. If I had that, I think I could handle almost anything.'

This was so absurd I had to step away from their door. I understand – really understand – why guys like Sima Qian's *Records of the Grand Historian*, or those silly action films from Toei V Cinema. Still, Satoru was a complete fraud. I remember him telling Koto how his parents were still crazy about each other, which totally enraptured Koto, who's in the middle of her own hot and heavy love affair. And how he told Naoki he went to the same elementary school and junior high as Naoki, and how they got all excited, going on and on about an old abandoned hospital in the neighbourhood. Who can tell what's true and what isn't?

I remembered Satoru's face, how he laughed the other day when he took me to the outdoor concert hall in Hibiya Park and said, 'I don't mind. I mean it's all made up anyway.' I don't think he meant any harm by it. He simply has no respect for the past. In that sense he's a lot like me. Still, he went too far – these false histories he was spouting were becoming way too convenient.

3.16

I was back from work and my legs were swollen from being on my feet all day, so I was stretched out on the floor, massaging them, when Koto came out of the girls' room, all fidgety, and started pacing back and forth between the living room and the kitchen.

'Could you be any more annoying?' I asked, and she came to a halt.

'How can you just sit there?' she asked and resumed pacing.

'What are you talking about?'

'Ryosuke's gone undercover, as we speak.'

Her words reminded me of this morning, when Ryosuke, tense and apparently not having slept a wink, emerged from the guys' room, eyes bloodshot, to complain that 'This is asking too much of me.' Their plan: he needed to go so far that he was assigned a girl, but then he could call it a day. He was supposed to come back without laying a finger on any of the girls, but seeing how on edge he was it looked like he had other ideas.

Right then there was a sound at the front door, and Koto leapt towards it. 'So how'd it go? He's busted, right?' I went to the entrance, half intrigued by the idea of seeing what kind of look Ryosuke would have on his face right after doing it with a girl.

Ryosuke looked at the two of us in turn, then shouted, 'That was no brothel!'

'What? It *wasn't*?' Koto asked.

'No way! It's a fortune teller's!'

'Are you kidding?'

'That guy is a fortune teller! He's famous among people who know about these things, and the word is his readings are always spot on. He only reads fortunes three days before and three days after a full moon or a new moon, and his readings for teenage girls and men in their sixties are especially right on target.'

As I listened to Ryosuke, half upset and half relieved at missing a chance to have sex on Koto's money, I burst out laughing.

According to Ryosuke, apartment 402 was dimly light with a red lamp or something. He was shown into a small room, sort of a reception area. A young woman was seated there. *Ah! This is the one I get to sleep with,* he was sure, trying to keep his heart from bursting from excitement. But then the man came in, asked him to write down his name and date of birth, and handed him a sheet of white paper. *Why do they need my name and date of birth for me to have sex with a woman?* Ryosuke wondered and decided it was best to write down phony information. Maybe because he was basically an honest guy, or maybe because he's a little slow on the uptake, but with the man watching him he couldn't for the life of him come up with a phony name and birth date. Panicking, he scribbled down Naoki's name and date of birth. When he finished, the man escorted him to a back room. There was a table with a crystal on it, and five or six cats at his feet.

'So – what? You're telling me you paid ¥20,000 and got Naoki's horoscope?' I asked, trying to keep from laughing again.

'Exactly! That's why I couldn't say no. What did you expect me to say? *Hey! Bring on the girl!?*'

Koto was so pale I figured she must be regretting the ¥20,000 she'd paid out of her pocket for a fortune-telling. 'Don't worry about it,' I consoled her. 'You can't get it back now.' It wasn't the money, though, but something else that had her so indignant.

'Since that dirty old man uses the place, does that mean that Japanese politics is being decided right next door to us?'

'I – guess so . . . That would make the guy next door Rasputin.'

Ryosuke was clearly regretting having wasted the money from Koto's meagre funds, and leapt at the chance of switching topics. I found the whole thing ridiculous and left. Back in the living room Ryosuke was launching into a discourse on the fall of the Russian Empire.

3.17

On the way back from work I stopped by a copy shop to pick up prints of my illustrations I'd had them do. Like always, I ended up complaining about how they used paper and colours other than the kind I'd told them to use. Why is it, I wondered, that the part-timers at the print shop always – and I mean *always* – do precisely what I tell them *not* to?

When I got back home, I was in a lousy mood, and Misaki was there for the first time in a while. It looked like she'd stopped by on her way home from work – she still had a suit on – and she was hanging out in the living room with Koto and Satoru.

The three of them were huddled together, still thinking up names for the shopping centre contest. The deadline was the next day.

'You're back early,' Misaki said to me. 'I was sure you'd be out drinking.'

I plopped down on the sofa. Satoru was seated next to me. He waved two pieces of paper in front of me, one with the words *K Road* written on it, the other with *Fernando Boulevard*. I flicked the one with *K Road* on it and said, 'Why Fernando?'

'It's the name of a Portuguese poet that Misaki likes,' Satoru explained.

'But why name a shopping district in Karasuyama after a poet you happen to like?' I asked, irritated.

'Satoru said we can choose any name,' Misaki pouted.

This had to be the first time she and Satoru had ever met each other, but the way they were huddled together like that, they looked like a pair of siblings.

'Does Naoki know you're here?' I asked, picking up the list of unlikely names they'd come up with.

'I called him earlier at work. I expect he'll be back soon.'

'Are you staying over?'

'I was planning to, but now I find that Satoru's taken over the sofa.' She didn't sound upset by it.

'Don't worry about me,' Satoru hurriedly said. 'I've got places I can stay for a night.'

'Why not sleep in Ryosuke's room?' Koto put in.

'No way, not that room,' Satoru said emphatically.

'How come?'

'Ryosuke keeps tossing and turning, and Naoki talks in his sleep. It's noisy.'

'I'd call it more creepy than noisy,' Misaki said, laughing.

Koto was looking in the direction of the front door, and it puzzled me. I saw she was reading the back of the piece of paper I was holding and I turned it over. It was a printed official warning about the serial attacks on young women in the neighbourhood. *Be Careful When You Walk Alone at Night!* it said.

The paper had a map of the area around the station, with Xs marking the places where the women had been attacked. The other day when the police had stopped by there'd been two attacks, but this paper had three Xs on it.

'They were handing these out at the station,' Misaki said and snatched the paper from me. 'It's dangerous, so you and Koto should be careful.'

'It's scary that they don't know anything about the attacker. I guess if he comes up behind them out of nowhere, there's no time to see his face.'

I grabbed the paper back from Misaki.

'Ah, that's right,' I said, 'I heard that the third woman who got attacked works part-time at that karaoke place – you know the one – in front of the Seiyu?'

As I said this, I remembered how Koto and I had gone to that karaoke place. 'Remember?' I went on. 'When the two of us went there, the girl at the register was supposed to give us back ¥2,000 in change but she almost handed us ¥20,000?'

Koto didn't seem too interested. 'Really? I don't remember,' she said.

'How do you know this?' Satoru asked me.

'The guy that works at the bento shop told me,' I replied.

According to the guy at the bento shop, the girl in this latest attack was hurt the worst of all. When she was found, unconscious, the girl's face was so deformed it was like her eyes, nose, and mouth had been moved around to different spots on her face. A bloody rock was found nearby.

In the middle of my explanation Satoru suddenly announced that he had to take a shower before going to work and disappeared into the bathroom.

After she watched him go, Misaki said, 'So he works?'

'Yeah, he does,' I answered.

'What kind of work could he be doing, this late at night?'

'I think he works in a bar or something,' Koto said.

'A bar? At his age?' Misaki's eyes widened exaggeratedly.

'You can work there when you're eighteen, right?' Koto replied.

'What? He's eighteen already?'

'How old did you think he was?' I asked.

Misaki glanced over at the bathroom. 'I was sure he was still about fifteen.'

'If you really thought he was fifteen,' I said, 'you should have wondered why he's living here before wondering about him working in a bar.'

'You've got a point.' Misaki gave a carefree laugh.

3.18

In the middle of the night I woke up with an awful feeling. I pulled the blanket up tight and closed my eyes again, but somehow I just couldn't get back to sleep. From below my bed I could hear Koto's regular, even breathing.

I got out of bed and quietly opened the door to the living room. From the gap in the curtains the street light outside shone in, and lit up Misaki's pale face as she slept on the sofa. 'I won't be back tonight,' Satoru had told her, 'so feel free to use the sofa.' He was nowhere to be seen.

After Satoru had left we waited for Naoki to come back from work, then all went out to a yakiniku restaurant. We ate and drank our fill and when we got back Ryosuke had returned from his part-time job. We ate the strawberries we'd bought on the way back from the restaurant, and drank wine until about one, then took turns showering, eventually heading to bed.

In the darkened living room I sat down next to Misaki, who was sound asleep, and picked up the piece of paper with the names for the shopping street that Koto and Satoru had come up with. I turned it over and held it up to the light. The thought that had suddenly struck me in bed wasn't a mistake after all. The first attack, along the train tracks of the Keio Line, where a twenty-two-year-old woman had been suddenly assaulted from behind by a man, her face smashed in, had taken place two months ago.

Holding the paper tight in my hand I went out of the living room, quietly so as not to waken Misaki, and opened the door to the guys' room. Ryosuke, as usual tossing and turning all night, hadn't just fallen out of his futon this time but had rolled over all the way to the door and lay right at my feet. I stepped over him and went in. Naoki, nestled in his loft-style bed, was breathing loudly, on the verge of snoring. I looked into his face, poked him softly on the cheek.

'Huh?' he said in a sleepy voice, then looked at me in surprise. 'Wh-what do you want?'

'Take a look at this,' I said, pulling the cord for the fluorescent light. A little light like this wasn't about to wake Ryosuke. Naoki blinked and took the paper from me.

'What is this?'

'Look at the date. Don't you notice something?' Naoki's expression stiffened when I said this.

'The date?'

'Look, it's nearly two months since the first attack.'

'Two months?'

'Right. Exactly the time that Satoru started living with us.'

'Satoru? Hold on. Didn't he come here more recently?'

'Are you sure?'

'I am. Man, what is with you?' Naoki said. 'And in the middle of the night, no less,' and he pulled the covers back up and shut his eyes.

Come to think of it, at the time of the third attack, five days ago, I was with Satoru the whole time. Our shop was closed for its regular day off and after going to an exhibition of Tibetan Buddhist art in Shibuya, I took him out drinking, against his will, not just to three a.m., when the attack occurred, but till four. I'm sure that was five days ago.

A little embarrassed, I quietly turned off the fluorescent light and exited the guys' room. I was cutting through the living room when Misaki, who I was sure was asleep, laughed. 'Been reading a lot of Misa Yamamura, have we?' she asked, naming a popular crime novelist.

Taken aback, I halted. 'I've never read her,' I said.

'Real life isn't like *Tuesday Suspense*,' she went on, 'where people are always getting entangled in crimes. Or are you thinking of accusing Satoru of being the criminal and chasing him out of here?'

After this, Misaki rolled over on the sofa and went back to sleep.

3.19

During the morning Misaki, who seemed on edge, announced that she wanted to go on a picnic, so she roused Ryosuke and Naoki from bed and we decided to go to Kinuta Park. It was the first time in a while that we'd all been together, so I was hoping Koto would join us, but she decided to stay home and wait for Satoru to return. 'I don't want to get sunburned,' she said, as an excuse. We told her to tell Satoru to come to the park if he came back before noon, then we all got into Ryosuke's Momoko. It had been ages since I'd taken a Sunday off from work.

Under the blue sky at the park, families sat on blankets on the almost dazzling green lawn, and little children scampered about. Ryosuke and Naoki immediately devoured over half of the sandwiches Koto had made for us, even though it wasn't yet lunchtime.

The four of us sprawled out on a mat for a while, then Misaki and Ryosuke starting playing catch with a pair of little twin boys whose ball had rolled our way. The twins, dressed in identical outfits, frolicked back and forth between Misaki and Ryosuke, screaming in delight. Naoki, sprawled out next to me on the mat, was watching them.

'You haven't told anybody what we talked about last night, have you?' I asked.

'Last night?'

'You know, about Satoru being the criminal . . .'

Naoki shot me a glance. 'Why would I?' he snorted derisively.

'I don't know, something just bugs me about it. I know he's not the criminal, but there's something that just doesn't smell right.'

'What do you mean – *something*?'

Naoki half sat up and poured some over-brewed jasmine tea from the thermos into a cup.

'I can't say, but something still bugs me.'

'*What?*'

'I told you – I can't explain it!'

'When you get right down to it, though, aren't you the one who brought Satoru home?'

'Well, you're right about that . . .'

Imagine somebody asking what kind of guy Satoru is. For her part Koto would probably say something like this:

'He's not very self-assertive. He's kind of laid-back, which makes me wonder if he's from a wealthy family. No matter what I invite him to do – pachinko, karaoke, bowling, whatever – he never says no. But he never seems to enjoy any of them. He just waits there, looking bored, until I suggest we go home. If I ask him if he is bored, he says, "Not really," and if I then ask if he's having fun I get the same reply – *Not really*. From what I hear, his parents are very much in love and he was raised very lovingly, so maybe he never felt greedy about anything growing up. Maybe people whose needs have always been met are like Satoru, very laid-back about life.'

Next is Ryosuke, who I imagine responding like this:

'He's so young, but he has no ambition. Look at me – I go to school, have a part-time job, go out with friends, put the moves on my friend's girlfriend, wash Momoko – there's never enough hours in the day. But Satoru wastes twenty hours every day. I think he has no ambition, though, because the guys he hangs out with have been such a bad influence. Most of them don't have steady jobs and they just sort of loiter around, so he turned out like them. Some people say that as long as you do your best you can do well in any circumstances, but I don't buy it. You can try your best, but if you're standing in mud you're going to fall. What Satoru needs is somebody to help drag him out of the mud.'

Both Koto and Ryosuke have already decided exactly who they think Satoru is – the kind of person they'd like to be with. And I think that Satoru, who is more streetwise than either of them, picks up on this and, in a sort of underhanded way, even, tries to pass himself off as the person they want him to be. Naturally, Koto and Ryosuke are also acting a part in their lives here. The same's true for me, and for Naoki. It's just that – how should I put it? – Satoru's a super-actor in a group of regular actors, a super-spectator among ordinary spectators. Somebody you just can't pin down, someone you try to touch but can't, like a reflection in a puddle. I can't help but see him that way.

On the lawn that stretches out before me Misaki and Ryosuke continued playing catch with the twin boys.

'Naoki – what do you think about Satoru?'

'What do you mean?' Naoki rolled over on the mat and there were blades of dried grass on his cheek.

'I mean, what kind of guy is he?'

'Just a typical young guy.'

'Really?'

'What're you getting at?'

'Well . . . I feel like Satoru isn't the kind of person Ryosuke thinks he is, or the kind Koto thinks he is. Not the kind you imagine him to be, and not even the kind of person I think he is.'

Before I'd finished Naoki turned away, disgusted, and squinted at the sun peeking through the clouds.

'That's pretty obvious,' he said.

'How come?'

I gave Naoki a little kick in the bum and he slowly sat up, rubbing his behind. 'The only Satoru you know is the one you know,' he said.

'What do you mean?'

'What I mean is, you only know the Satoru you know. In the same way, I only know the Satoru I know. Ryosuke and Koto, too, only know the Satoru they know.'

'I don't get it *at all.*'

'Nobody knows the Satoru that all of us knows. That guy doesn't exist.'

Naoki pulled out a BLT from the lunchbox and happily chomped down on it, getting ketchup on his lips.

'Hold on – you going to leave it at that? That's gibberish.'

I gave Naoki another kick in the behind.

'Do you know what a multiverse is?'

'Never heard of it. What is it?'

'You've heard of a universe, right?'

'Sure.'

'Multiverse means multiple universes.'

'Okay . . .'

So what? I was about to shoot back, but held back, because I sort of understood what he was getting at. Sometimes I hear this pseudo-humanitarian line that goes *In this world everyone's a star.* If that's true, then everyone's the star in *all the worlds* that make up *this world,* and if everyone's a star, in effect that's the same as if no one is a star. That would make it an equal world, close to the kind of life the five of us are living now. But strictly speaking, in order to get to a world where no one is the star, you need for the world to be such that everyone can be a star . . . Hmmm . . . I guess I don't get it.

3.20

'My wisdom teeth are really pushing through my gums these days,' Naoki said, lying on the mat with his mouth wide open.

His tongue was red, like it was dyed by the sun. 'Let me see!' Misaki, Ryosuke, and I said, peering in turn into his mouth. You could see a white, protruding object bulging out through the gums.

'Does it hurt?'

'Sometimes.'

Misaki stuck her finger into his mouth and went right ahead and pushed his cheek out. A thought suddenly came to me: the two of them used to be lovers.

Come to think of it, when Ryosuke went undercover next door at apartment 402 and had Naoki's fortune read instead of his, the fortune teller told him, 'You have a great desire for a change . . .

In seeking change you're struggling against the world.' Looking at this guy sprawled out on the grass at Kinuta Park, with mouth wide open like an idiot, his Adam's apple sticking out, I don't know what kind of world he's struggling against, though he's definitely at war with one thing – his wisdom teeth.

At the end of his fortune-telling the Rasputin next door apparently said this: 'If you break out of this world you'll find this world again, only one size larger. In your struggle with the world, the world has the advantage.'

As the fortune teller was seeing Ryosuke out he added, 'If you're interested, next time I'll tell *your* fortune.' The fortune itself was too abstract to make much sense, but seeing as how he saw right through Ryosuke, perhaps we wasn't a phony fortune teller after all.

SATORU KOKUBO (18)

4.1

Last night Misaki, Naoki's old girlfriend, showed up. So there's one more person in this group of people-playing-at-being-friends. A nutcase girl who comes up with a name like 'Fernando Boulevard' for the Karasuyama shopping district. Apparently their apartment was originally rented by Naoki and this nutty girl. A cowardly college student. A love-addicted girl. A freelance illustrator who likes to hang out with gay guys. And a health-obsessed jogger. If I hadn't met them there, there's no way I would ever talk to people like that. Still, hanging out with them turns out to be more fun than I ever imagined.

Last night I let this new girl, Misaki, have the sofa. Then I went out to Shinjuku, after ten, and Makoto and I did our usual thing, taking speed in a public toilet and then hanging out, high, in the park. In less than five minutes this guy who stuck his tongue out like a lizard picked up Makoto, and I figured this night I was out of luck, but then Sylvia, a regular customer, picked me up.

For whatever reason, ever since I started living in that apartment customers haven't been biting.

I went with Sylvia – who's shooting up so many hormones she's pretty emotionally unstable – to her place, serviced her, and finally fell asleep near dawn, but still woke up at eleven, had one of her Calorie Mate bars for lunch, and left. I was wandering in the direction of Hatagaya Station when I saw a young girl exiting a high-end condo, the kind with a self-locking front door. Her profile reminded me a bit of Koto. The girl checked her mailbox, which had the number of her apartment on it, dumped a sack of rubbish, and walked off towards the station.

I bought a hot dog and milk at a convenience store, sat on some railings, and kept an eye on the condo. When a young guy, college student by the look of him, came out, I slipped inside just before the front door locked. I went to the seventh floor and with the handy wire I always carry with me, prised open the door to her place in under two minutes.

The apartment was neat and tidy. The pillows were in a strange location, but the bed was nicely made, and the dried flowers hanging on the wall smelled like lavender. A pair of flesh-coloured stockings were discarded on the bed, perhaps because they had runs in them, one stocking hung down towards the wooden floor. There was a burnt smell of butter and toast, probably the remains of breakfast. A typical studio apartment with white walls and wooden flooring.

I took a look around the place, went back down the short hallway to the front door. I locked it and lined up my trainers, which I'd been carrying, next to some black pumps.

In the middle of the apartment was a low table. This girl who resembled Koto must have had some tea before she left – there was a mug with a tiny amount of tea in the bottom. I carefully lifted the cup up and carried it to the kitchen. Running the tap just a little so as not to splash any water, I rinsed the cup in the sink, and poured in some hot water from a push-button carafe. There wasn't much left in it – it spat out hot water, scalding my fingers, and I shrieked out in pain, my voice reminding me of Sylvia's voice last night, which sort of left me stunned.

I found some Lipton tea bags on top of the fridge. I steeped a tea bag in the hot water, swinging it back and forth. The clear hot water turned a murky red and a sweet fragrance rose up.

Come to think of it, no one in that apartment drinks tea. Koto, Mirai, and Ryosuke are all coffee drinkers, while health-nut Naoki drinks alcohol but still insists that coffee and cigarettes are the *devil's favourites*.

I left the cup with the tea in the sink and went into the bedroom. I looked outside through a gap in the light pink curtains and could see the skyscrapers of Shinjuku off in the distance, and right in front of them the Metro Expressway. I heard from Ryosuke that it's nearly ten kilometres from Chitose Karasuyama to Shinjuku. On his days off Naoki's been known to take a train to Shinjuku and then jog all the way back home.

From the seventh floor of this girl's apartment it was easy to see the traffic-clogged motorway. The double glazing, though, muffled any sound. It was like the sound had been completely removed from the city.

On the wooden window frame were little figurines of Snow White's Seven Dwarfs. When I counted the dwarfs, though, there were only six of them. Thinking I must have knocked one down, I checked under my feet, and underneath the bed, but no luck – the missing dwarf remained missing.

I picked up one of the dwarfs, with its orange hat, and lined it up against the city streets outside. The dwarf trampled down the skyscrapers and steel towers, just like Godzilla. The brick condos, the Takefuji billboard – the dwarf, beaming all the while, crushed them all underfoot.

There was an alarm clock next to the bed. I picked it up and saw that it was set to ring at ten a.m. I set it to the present time, two p.m., and this silly voice called out 'Get up! Get up!' over and over, then changed to a barking dog. I sniggered, set the time back to ten and put the clock back where it was.

I put the hot dog and milk I bought at the convenience store out on the table. The guy at the store must have zapped the hot dog too long in the microwave since it was all shrunk in the wrapper. I bit down on it and the sweet fat slowly spread to the back of my throat.

There was a Polaroid camera on top of the fourteen-inch TV. With the hot dog in one hand, in the other I grabbed the camera and looked through the lens at the room around me. The room seemed larger than when seen with the naked eye. Suddenly, I got the feeling like somebody was standing there, just outside the square frame of the lens, and I hurriedly pulled my eye away from it. Nobody was there, of course. It's like with a twenty-four-frame roll of film there's somebody on the twenty-fifth frame, on a thirty-six-frame roll, somebody on the thirty-seventh.

Next to the TV was a bag from a video rental place, a chain store that has a branch in Chitose Karasuyama too. I peeked in the bag and found a copy of the film *Pink Panther 2*. I've heard of it but have never seen it.

I stuck the video in the deck, switched on the TV and quickly lowered the volume. I leaned back against the bed, stretched out my feet, all prepared to enjoy the film. In a sort of museum, this Arab guide with a phony-looking moustache is explaining about this diamond with sparkling bluish highlights to a large group of visitors. I turned up the volume a little.

This is the Pink Panther, he says, *symbol of our people for the last thousand years since the Akbar Dynasty. It is the largest and best-known diamond in the world. A unique, priceless gem.*

Aren't you afraid it will be stolen? one of the visitors asks. The guide slowly reaches out towards the display of the diamond. Immediately a shrill alarm pierces the air and heavy steel shutters slam shut on the windows of the museum.

Why is it called the Pink Panther? another visitor asks.

The guide smugly replies, *It's called that because if you shine a light on it from a certain angle it looks like a pink panther is dancing inside.*

As the guide explains this, the camera zooms up on the diamond and the famous theme song, which I've heard before, begins, and an animated pink panther begins to gyrate around in a dance.

Just then, the phone rang. I hurriedly switched off the TV. The phone rang five times, then went to voicemail. As the recorded message started up I realised I didn't need to panic and I plonked myself back down again. A girl's sugary voice started up on the message.

'Hi – this is Maki. Sorry I backed out of the party with Takahashi and the others last Saturday! It must be your lunch break now so I was going to phone you at work or your mobile, but you know how chicken I am – I was afraid you'd get upset so I called your home instead. If you hear this and think you might forgive me, I'll be at home tonight so please give me a call. But if you get angry all over again when you hear this, it'll be too scary for me, so please don't call me. When you get angry it really does frighten me . . .'

Before I'd realised what I was doing, I was crouched down like a cat, face to face with the phone. The red message light was blinking.

'. . . And I'd like to see the Hong Kong video, so could you lend it to me? Be careful not to record a SMAP x SMAP variety show over it like you did with the Hawaii video. You know, you should snap off the safety tab . . .'

Right then the buzzer buzzed, the dial tone came on, and the phone call abruptly ended. Thinking she might call back I stood there, cat-like with my rear end stuck out, but the phone didn't ring again.

I looked up at the shelf of videotapes and next to a video of a live Dragon Ash concert was one labelled *Hong Kong 2001*. I took out the *Pink Panther* tape and slipped it in the machine. After some static, this room came on the screen. For a second I almost ran off to the front door. It was like there was a hidden camera somewhere in here that had suddenly sprung to life and was filming this very room. But what was on screen wasn't this room in real time, with me in it. Instead of me, crouched there like a feline, there was a large suitcase in the same spot.

The scene changed to the view out of the window, then panned to the kitchen. The girl who had just exited this building, the one who looked like Koto, was washing dishes. She must have just taken a shower since she had a bath towel wrapped around her hair, and a toothbrush sticking out of her mouth.

Just to make double sure, I looked over at the kitchen – naturally there wasn't a girl standing there with a bath towel wrapped around her hair.

The girl taking the video seemed to be talking so I turned up the volume a little. When the scale got to sixteen I could make out what she was saying.

We don't have time. Forget about the dishes, dry your hair instead.

The girl who resembled Koto went on washing the dishes, glanced at the camera, and mumbled – still with the toothbrush in her mouth – *Bring that dirty glass over here, will you?*

With a soapy finger she pointed to the table and I instinctively glanced down. Not surprisingly, there wasn't any dirty glass on it.

As I watched the video for a while I figured out that the girl who looked like Koto, the one washing the dishes, was named Yuko, while the one taking the video was Maki, the one who'd called a few minutes ago. After Maki brought the dirty glass over to the kitchen, she continued filming Yuko's hands as she washed the dishes.

The more I watched this, the more it felt like Yuko and Maki were actually here in the apartment with me. If I looked over I would see Yuko doing the dishes in the kitchen and Maki videoing her . . . But they weren't there. All I saw was the untouched mug filled with tea.

About five minutes later the scene abruptly changed from this apartment to a view of Hong Kong at night. Growing tired of watching any more alone, I brought the dwarfs over and lined them up on the table facing the TV.

The scene on the video was taken from the window of a high-rise hotel, the typical night scene of Hong Kong you see on TV and postcards, the water of the harbour undulating down below.

The camera turned and the girl who looked like Koto was sprawled out on a sofa in the hotel room. I waited for a while, thinking she was going to say something, but then that scene cut off. *It comes with a lid!* a voice said as the next scene started, taken during the day in a shopping district with rows of gaudy signs, then this scene, too, abruptly stopped.

The rest of the scenes were all short, and in none of them did Yuko and Maki sound very happy. Instead, a spiritless voice – one of theirs – mixed in with the Hong Kong scenery, was saying things like *I'm worn out. You want to go back to the hotel?* With these muttered words the scene cut off.

Totally bored, I hit Fast Forward. One scene of Hong Kong after another flashed by and when the video counter got to twenty-four minutes the screen suddenly went dark. And just as quickly another scene came on, of Yuko in her underwear. I hurriedly hit Play.

The scene was in the same hotel room as the beginning. When I rewound it and watched again, Yuko was coming out of the bathroom, in her black underwear, saying *Hey! Don't film me!* and then slipping on a shiny red dress that was spread out on the sofa.

That looks great on you. How much was it? Maki's voice says.

Yuko mumbled a reply I couldn't catch it. Wearing the red dress now, Yuko walked towards the camera, like she was going to leap out of the screen and appear right before me. The whole screen turned red with the dress, then as she got even closer, it went black. Yuko slowly twirled around in front of the camera, playfully stuck her bum out and then moved away towards the bed.

I couldn't take my eyes off the scene. Before I realised it, I'd knocked two of the dwarfs off the table.

The Hong Kong video ended with that scene. I kept on fast-forwarding, but that was it. I rewound to the scene with Yuko in her underwear. I paused the part where she stuck her rear end out at the camera. A tiny bit of flab seeped over her black panties. Maybe it was because I'd paused that frame, but her flesh seemed to jiggle.

I lay down on Yuko's bed, doing my best not to wrinkle the bedspread. Last night Sylvia had squeezed everything out of my cock, but it was almost painfully erect again. It was nearly bursting through the denim of my jeans, and I could feel it pulsing. The room was as still as always. I couldn't hear a sound from outside, either. Just the alarm clock ticking away.

I unzipped and my cock sprang out. I picked up the Polaroid camera from the table and snapped a photo of my hard-on. For an instant the flash lit up the room.

Once I asked Ryosuke how he took care of business. I mean, he shared a room with Naoki, and Koto was always in the living room. Ryosuke began by saying, 'Now don't ever tell anybody about this, okay?' and went on to explain. 'There's a playground behind the building, right? I go there and do it in the toilets.' According to him, this life where he can't even freely masturbate 'doesn't particularly bother' him.

On the black Polaroid the outline of my cock began to emerge. In the background was the empty kitchen. Unlike the photo, my cock had now wilted and I stuffed it back into my underpants. I glanced at the clock and it had been two hours since I snuck in.

I got up off the bed and smoothed out the wrinkles. I turned off the TV and the video and put the *Hong Kong 2001* and *Pink Panther 2* videos back where they belonged. I returned the dwarfs back to the windowsill, stowed the milk and hotdog leftovers in the convenience store plastic bag, and put the Polaroid camera back on the table.

The tea I hadn't drunk was completely cold. I poured it down the sink, leaving a little bit in the bottom of the cup, and put the cup back on the table.

I looked around the apartment. Everything was the same as

when I came in. The only thing different was the red message light flashing.

As I walked to the front door I gave the place another once-over, but couldn't find anything out of place. When I'd first snuck in, the apartment looked very appealing, but in two hours' time I was bored with it. I hardly ever find a place I'd like to stay in for long.

I slipped out of the building, trying to keep out of sight. On the way to Hatagaya Station I felt like calling the apartment, so I stopped by a public phone and made the call. As expected, Koto answered.

'Oh – it's you,' she said, obviously disappointed.

'Where is everybody?' I asked.

'They went on a picnic at Kinuta Park,' she answered, sounding bored by it.

'Misaki, too?'

'Yeah. Misaki, Naoki, and Mirai all went in Ryosuke's Momoko on a picnic.'

'Why didn't you go with them?'

'I don't want to get a sunburn.'

'So what are you up to now?'

'Nothing, really. What about you? Where are you?'

'I'm in Hatagaya. Is Misaki staying over at our place tonight, too?'

'She said she's going home. She said Ryosuke was going to give her a lift on his way to work.'

'I guess I'll go home then.'

'Yes, come on home. Let's watch some videos together.'

'Videos? . . . Like what, for instance?'

'I don't care. Pick up something on your way back.'

'There's nothing I particularly want to see . . . Oh – have you ever seen *The Pink Panther*?'

'*The Pink Panther*? No, I haven't . . . That's fine with me. Are you going to work tonight?'

'Tonight? . . . I might take the night off. I worked too hard yesterday.'

'Then get two videos, okay?'

As I was about to hang up Koto yelled out, 'And get some doughnuts from that shop near the station!'

4.2

I was slumped on the sofa, wrapped in a blanket, spreading strawberry jam on a waffle that Koto made me when Naoki came in and said, 'Satoru, you feel like working at my company today?'

Of course I didn't, so I said no and bit into the hot waffle. Koto was already making another batch of waffles. 'You should do it,' she said, so I asked Naoki what sort of work it was. He works at a film distribution company and all they wanted was someone to stick labels on envelopes with announcements of a preview showing of their next film. A simple enough job, but since they were talking about several hundred envelopes it wasn't the kind of work that could be finished in an hour or two. The other employees were all busy preparing for the Cannes Film Festival and the films they were going to buy to distribute, so no one else could help out.

'You're taking the day off anyway, right?' Naoki asked as he bit into a waffle of his own.

'I haven't decided,' I replied, but it didn't look like the listlessness I'd been feeling the last few days was going to vanish by evening.

In the end, with Koto egging me on, I showered and went along with Naoki. The inside of the train was mobbed, and by the time we got to Yotsuya, where his company was, I was exhausted.

In the train Naoki asked me, 'Are you going to quit the job you have now?' I didn't reply and he went on: 'It's okay to quit, but you can't just leave things unclear like this. You've got to sit down and have a talk with your boss.'

'What should I talk to him about?' I asked.

'Tell him when you're planning to quit. He's got to have time to find a replacement. Right?'

It seemed like Mirai hadn't told anybody what sort of work I do. I held on to a strap to keep from falling over under the weight of an old guy pressed up against me, and as I did so, the faces of Sylvia and other clients came to mind.

This is my last month standing here, folks. Next week I'll have a closing-down sale, so all services are half price.

Naoki's company was on the sixth floor of a multi-purpose office building. Inside were tall stacks of metal film reel containers, and boxes of pamphlets and leaflets pressed up against them, as if to keep them from falling over.

'Good morning!' Naoki called out through gaps in the stacks as he strode into the office, and behind a partition pasted over with notices a voice called out, 'Ihara, is that you?' It was an older woman's voice, slightly panicky.

'Good morning!' Naoki said again, and peeked behind the partition. 'What's going on?' he asked. I hadn't known Naoki's last name up till then – Ihara.

'Nothing really. They say we can get an interview with Woody Allen,' the hidden voice said, almost screaming it out.

'Are you kidding? Where?' Naoki motioned to me to come over.

'In Munich.'

'Munich? When?'

'Next week. Are you free then? Momochi can't make it, and Satoko and Mitchan will be in San Francisco . . . What should we do?'

Naoki listened to her, then pulled me by the hand and pushed me behind the partition. There were four desks there, all piled high with papers. At the furthest desk sat a middle-aged woman wearing a pair of gaudy glasses. She was the head of the company.

'This is my cousin,' Naoki said. 'I brought him over to help paste labels for the invitations to the preview.'

Since he introduced me, I gave a little bow of greeting. In spite of her appearance, the woman's smile was warm and friendly. 'Really?' she said. 'That's great. What's your name?' 'Satoru,' I replied, then quickly added 'Kokubo'. The woman owner and Naoki continued their conversation. There was no one else in the little office.

Sipping the coffee she'd made for me, I sat down at a desk near the entrance and, following Naoki's directions, started pasting on address labels. It was for the film *London Dogs*, with Jude Law, a favourite of my customers these days. Behind the partition the intense conversation between the two of them went on, constantly interrupted by incoming phone calls.

'Momochi's in charge of this, right? I heard he was turned down for an exclusive interview in New York, though . . .'

'He got in touch with the agent many times, but they've already started the next film.'

'I see . . . I'd still like to get an interview with the director, though,' the woman owner said.

'I know what you mean. Momochi asked me to get *Cut* to let

us put an article in their next issue, the special on New York. It'd
be great to get an interview with the director. But why Munich?'

'They're premiering in Europe this month, so he went to Munich
for that and stayed for a holiday.'

'How much do you think we could get to cover it?'

'Well, we'd need a writer and a photographer, but if possible
I'd like to get by without an interpreter.'

'I've got someone in mind. You remember Hanawa, who we
brought for the MIFED film festival? His English is pretty
good . . .'

As he spoke with the woman president of the company Naoki
briskly handled the incoming calls, sometimes answering in fluent
English. I wanted to see what sort of expression he had when he
spoke English, so I peeked over the partition. He was leaning back
in his chair, didn't look tense at all, and when he saw me he
motioned with his hand for me to *Get back to work!*

To tell the truth, Naoki looked pretty cool. For the first time in
my life I even thought I might want to wear a tie. I wonder – have
Mirai and Koto and Ryosuke ever seen Naoki like this? I remember
how they said Ryosuke got Naoki's fortune read by the fortune
teller next door. It was something absurd about *fighting with the
world* – it made me laugh when I heard it – but when I see him
working here he really is – unlike me – battling with a huge world
out there.

They had all sorts of small errands to do. I had to move, since
they needed the space to lay out some materials, and then they
sent me to the post office to mail some things, so it was past two-
thirty by the time I finished pasting all the labels.

Naoki said he'd buy me lunch and took me to a nearby ramen
shop. When I told him, honestly, that I'd been impressed, he was

clearly flattered and said, 'I've liked films since I was a kid, and it's great to be able to earn a living at a job I enjoy so much.

'By the way,' he went on, 'what do you plan to do with your life?'

The sudden question threw me, and a bite of seafood fried rice stuck in my throat. This might have been the first time since junior high that someone asked me what I wanted to do in the future. I was beyond yelling out *I want to be a pilot! Or a doctor!*

'Me?'

'You must have some idea, right? You're working at a bar, so maybe you want to open your own place someday?'

'My own place?'

I was silent after that, and Naoki looked like he was struggling with whether he should say anything more. He was staring straight at me.

'What?' I asked him.

'Uh – nothing,' he said, awkwardly. It seemed for a second that he might be wondering whether he should ask me what I do to earn a living. Mirai probably didn't tell them because she figured they weren't the type of people to approve of what I do.

'What? What is it?' This was bothering me and I asked Naoki again, as he slurped up his tan-tan men noodles. Again he said, 'It's nothing,' but then immediately raised his head and looked right into my eyes.

'Are you – by any chance . . .'

'What are you getting at?'

'Did you run away from home?'

'What?'

'I figured you'd run away from home, and that's why you sleep at different places. I don't know why you ran away, but I do think you should give your folks a call. Parents get worried, you know. If it's . . . hard for you to call yourself, I could call for you.'

I looked at Naoki, slurping his noodles, and thought how usually we act like friends together, but he is, after all, a twenty-eight-year-old fart. But while part of me was mocking him, I admit I also felt like I should thank him for being willing to do something like that for me. It was a weird feeling. It seems like before I even realised it, I've become a card-carrying member of their Let's-Play-Friends game.

Anyhow, I told him I hadn't run away, and Naoki just said, 'Is that right?' and drained back the thick soup in his bowl.

On the way back to his office maybe he still suspected I was a runaway 'cause he started telling me how he'd run away from home himself when he was fifteen.

'So even a person like you runs away from home?' I said.

'What does that mean?' Naoki laughed.

He ran away in the winter, just after he turned fifteen. He was planning to hitchhike, but his fussiness and the cold winter wind made him give up on standing beside the road. Instead, he took a train headed towards Yatsugatake.

'Why did you run away?' I asked.

'Why? I was fifteen, come on.'

'That's a reason? That doesn't explain anything.'

'Really? I thought it would.'

Naoki told me if I was finished pasting labels I could leave, but somehow I found it hard to and tagged along back to the company. I helped with filing and making copies until about six p.m., when Naoki's senior colleague, Momochi, came back.

I went home that night feeling sort of energetic after working, and just as I got home Ryosuke was setting out for his part-time job.

'You going to work tonight?' he asked me. 'I'll give you a lift to Shinjuku.' I told him to wait and phoned Makoto's home, but he said he didn't have any speed on him. 'I'm going to take the night off,' I told Ryosuke, who was tugging on his shoes at the entrance.

Apparently Ryosuke was going to stop by Kiwako's place after work. As I saw him off I asked, 'Are things going okay with her?' and he said, all carefree, 'Not bad.'

'Not bad? You're still on the fence about her, I'm betting,' I laughed.

'Don't be so sarcastic.'

'But it's the truth.'

'I hate that word.'

'What word?'

'Truth. I don't feel any truth in it.'

With this, Ryosuke set out happily for his part-time job. The other day when Koto asked him, 'When you're with Kiwako do you guys ever talk about Umezaki?' Ryosuke calmly replied, 'We do. Actually, when I'm with her, that's all we ever talk about.' I don't know why I suddenly remembered that.

Koto was apparently out on a date with Tomohiko Maruyama, and Mirai wasn't back yet. As I sat on the living-room sofa I realised for the first time that I was all by myself.

Not like I was digging into things or anything, but as I like to do, I went into the girls' room and started opening the dresser and desk drawers. Just like I'd heard, all of Koto's possessions were stuffed in three small cardboard boxes neatly placed next to the bed. On the walls were several framed illustrations of Mirai's. The other day she'd photographed me to help with her drawings, and took photos of my chin and ears, back and thighs, finally even snapping photos of my bum.

I opened the wardrobe and pulled out a stack of boxes. One of them had winter jumpers that Mirai had been wearing until not long ago, and when I pulled out one white jumper to get a closer look something fell out. It seemed like a video tape. It was inside a plastic bag from a convenience store, and was taped tightly shut. I had to see what was inside so I careful unpeeled the tape, and discovered an ordinary 120-minute Sony video. Porn? I wondered. I went back to the living room right away and inserted the tape into the tape deck.

The tape, surprisingly, had parts that were blurred out. But it wasn't porn, just an ordinary film. I watched it for a while – what film it was I had no idea – and then it abruptly switched to another film. Then another scene came on, this one, too, showing a girl getting raped. I fast-forwarded and found yet another rape scene. Seemed that she'd spliced together a bunch of rape scenes from different films.

'God, what awful taste,' I muttered and switched off the tape. Was this also something to help with her illustrations? I wondered, and as I watched the blank TV screen a chill shot up my spine. I suddenly felt like a terrible smell was drifting out to the living room from those illustrations of Mirai's hanging on the wall. And that smell was, without a doubt, semen. That strong odour that sticks to your thighs and belly and chest, that you wash and wash and can't get rid of.

Back when I was just starting out trolling for customers at the park and I hadn't yet got the hang of things, I used to lie next to the customers for a while once we were done. I can't believe I used to do that. My clients used to talk about all kinds of things. Mostly it was bragging about how popular they used to be when they were young. But one of them told me about a murder that

took place in a village in France a long time ago. I can't remember
the guy's face, but for some reason I remember every detail of the
story he told me.

A long time ago there was a young boy named Pierre in a remote
village in France. There were five people in his family: his wimpy
father, his evil mother, a younger sister, and an infant brother.
Pierre used to talk to the cabbages in the fields, even debate with
them at times, sometimes beating them with a cane or umbrella.
But he loved his faint-hearted father deeply.

Pierre's mother looked down on her husband. You're a good-
for-nothing, spineless wimp, she told him, treating him little better
than a donkey. Pierre's mean younger sister took her mother's side.
Pierre couldn't stand to watch how his father was mistreated by
his wife and daughter.

His father worked hard every single day, and Pierre helped him
out as best he could. His father doted on his baby son. His wife
and daughter might overwork him, but his father just kept on,
never complaining, all for the sake of his beloved baby son. And
Pierre, too, naturally loved his baby brother from the bottom of
his heart.

The tragedy took place one day when Pierre's father was gone
out to work. In order to free his father from this living hell, Pierre
killed his mother as she was cooking porridge on the stove. He
stabbed her in the neck and head. His sister tried to run away but
he killed her in the garden. His sister, clutching some lace she
had been knitting, was repeatedly stabbed in the face and neck.
Then, after Pierre went back into the house, he stabbed his baby
brother, in his cradle, in the back.

Pierre was on the run for some time, but was finally caught.
When asked by the prosecutor why he would kill his beloved baby

brother, Pierre, drained of all spirit, replied, 'I was afraid that if I had just killed my mother and sister and had spared my brother, even if my father was afraid of my actions, when I was executed for what I'd done for him he would have been full of regret. So I killed my beloved brother as well. That way my father would be happy to see me die, wouldn't be sad at my death at all, and could live a happier life than before.'

I have no idea why, right after I saw Mirai's video tape, I recalled this story. But I just couldn't shake the mental image of Pierre that I'd created.

Next to Mirai's bed was a photo of her, her arms around Mariné Mama, beaming at the camera, with a couple of gay guys around her. There was one night, I recall, when Mirai and I were out drinking and she'd had so much she couldn't stand up. One of the gay guys and I propped her up, muttering what a pain in the bum she was, but she just yelled out, in high spirits, that we should all go to *one more bar!*

As I sat next to her bed, gazing at the photo, I wondered if there was something I could do for her. And then realised right away that there wasn't. Honestly, I didn't think there was anything I could do for anybody.

I went back to the living room and was taking Mirai's video tape out of the deck but I pushed the button for the other video deck by mistake. There are two decks side by side, one Naoki's, the other Mirai's. The tape that came out of the other deck was the one Koto and I had watched the other day, *The Pink Panther.*

I don't know where the idea came from, but by the time I realised what I was doing, I'd recorded the scene of the animated pink panther dancing onto Mirai's rape scene video.

I rewound it and played it again. Instead of the rape scenes there was the pink panther prancing around, the same scene over and over. Sometimes, though, as soon as the panther's dance finished, for an instant there'd be a woman's contorted face on the screen.

4.3

Last night I went to the park for the first time in a long while. It rained in the evening, and it was warm and muggy, so business was good. In the morning I was going to take the first train, but going back home to Chitose Karasuyama seemed like too much trouble, so I stayed over at a sauna in Kabukicho. I went into the dry sauna three times, for seven minutes each, scrubbed myself well twice with a scrub cloth, took a cold bath, then went to the nap room to sleep.

A guy sleeping in the corner of the nap room woke me up with his snoring, and I left the sauna before noon, went to a Lotteria and ordered a shrimp burger. The films were about to start at the nearby cinemas and the place was packed with moviegoers trying to fill their stomachs before the show began. There was an empty seat at the counter so I went over there, tray in hand, and sat down. Next to me were two older men, munching on teriyaki burgers and complaining how they gave them heartburn the rest of the day.

The piped-in music in the place was loud and I could only catch snatches of their conversation. For some reason, though, the guy in the cloth cap next to me came through loud and clear when he said, 'You know, my wife passed away two years ago.'

He went on, deprecatingly, saying, 'Now that I'm by myself the house seems so big. And since I'm at home all day, it seems even bigger.'

'I wonder about that,' the other guy said. 'Seems to me you're living it up, Mr Takashina. Look at me – it's me and my wife together all day long. If I don't get out sometimes and stroll around Shinjuku I feel like I'm going to suffocate.'

Curious, I turned to look at this man in the cloth cap, Mr Takashina, seated next to me. Crazy long eyebrows, a worn-out old cap, salt-and-pepper sideburns. Liver spots on his cheeks.

'Since the end of last year I started delivering newspapers,' the one called Takashina said. If I concentrated really hard, I could make out what the two of them were saying.

'Delivering newspapers?'

'Yeah. I wake up early anyway, and the newspaper shop's right next door, so I asked the manager and he has me deliver to thirty houses every morning.'

'Thirty?'

'It only takes twenty to thirty minutes, but it makes me feel good the rest of the day.'

'Isn't it cold in the winter?'

'When there's snow on the ground I tell them I'm afraid of falling and take the day off.'

Half listening to the two men's conversation, I finished my shrimp burger and fries. I stood up to leave but they stood up at the same instant, so I sat down in a nearby chair and watched them as they left.

The two men exchanged a few words outside the shop and then went their separate ways. I left the shop and, without much thought, started following Takashina, the one who delivered newspapers.

Gazing up at the marquees along the row of cinemas in Kabukicho, Takashina made one circuit of the square. I stood in the middle of the square and watched him as he made one complete round. I suddenly realised that the place was filled with men his age, walking alone, out to see a film in the morning.

Takashina finally settled on *Hannibal*. I lined up behind him as he bought a ticket and followed him inside the cinema. It was still lit up and he walked to the front, to the back again, then the front, unable to decide where to sit. I stood by the door, watching him trying to decide, until he picked out a seat in the very front row, so close he could almost touch the screen if he stretched out his legs.

I sat down two rows behind him and watched the movie. I hadn't slept well at the sauna's nap room, so I dozed off a bit during the film, but as advertised it was grotesque and interesting. At the end when Lecter broke open a man's skull and was scooping out and eating his brains, I nearly yelled out. I looked at Mr Takashina two rows ahead of me and he was also leaning forwards, glued to the screen.

When he left the cinema he made straight for Shinjuku Station. He cut through the crowded concourse inside the station and went through the turnstile to the Odakyu Line.

The train he took was a local one that left two minutes later. It wasn't exactly packed, but there weren't any seats left. Next to the door was a 'silver seat' reserved for the elderly, and a young guy, a college student by the look of him, gave up this seat to Mr Takashina. The train set off and Mr Takashina was lost in a pamphlet he was reading.

I stood right in front of him, holding on to a strap, and could see what he was reading. He raised his head once and shot me a look, but he didn't seem to remember me sitting right next to him in the Lotteria a few hours before.

The first time I snuck into another person's house was when I was five. My father was unemployed then and the two of us were living in public housing in Tama New Town. It was a Sunday and my father was watching a golf tournament on TV. He dozed off and when he woke up it was dark outside and he suddenly realised his little boy was no longer next to him. Not that worried, he figured I was playing in the corridor outside or on the stairs and he went out to look for me. I often played on the landing, but this time he didn't find me there.

Panicking, my father went around the perimeter of the building – at this time of evening nice cooking smells were coming out of the units – calling out my name. The housewives on the estates were a tightly knit group, and as soon as they heard my father calling out for me, they quickly got together and broke into teams to search – one team searching the park, one the riverbank, another group to keep in touch with the designated fire monitor in each building. They ignored my father and quickly assembled a search party that scoured the grounds of the estate, flashlight beams arcing back and forth in the gathering gloom.

While all this was going on, I was in the apartment of a newly married couple one floor below. The couple had gone out and had apparently forgotten to lock up. I snuck inside, watched TV, and had fallen asleep.

It was after ten p.m. when they found me. The search outside had got pretty large-scale, I heard later, with several policemen involved. Naturally the first ones who found me were the young couple, back from shopping in a department store in Ginza, loaded down with shopping bags. They parked their car and found everyone in the estate tense, searching for the lost boy. The young wife had apparently seen me before, playing on the stairs and landing, and despite being tired out from shopping all day, she told the head of the local women's association that she would help search as soon as she put away her bags. She rushed into her apartment.

As the young wife ran up the stairs she found her husband standing at their front door. 'It isn't locked,' he told her. 'That can't be,' she replied. 'It's true.' 'You were the last one out.' 'No, *you* were.' They argued their way inside. Pale light from the TV filtered out in the dark apartment, and they were startled for a second. And there, on the floor, bathed in the pale light, was a little boy, face up, sound asleep.

Mr Takashina got off at a station called Soshigaya Okura, directly south of where Chitose Karasuyama would be if you were on the Keio Line.

Leaving the station, Mr Takashina leisurely strolled towards a long line of shops radiating off from the station, and stopped inside a supermarket with mounds of Florida oranges at the entrance. I thought of following him but decided to wait outside and have a smoke. It was about twenty minutes later that he came out, carrying plastic shopping bags in both hands. He glanced at me for an instant, a brief look of doubt in his eyes. But then, apparently untroubled, he continued walking down the shopping district.

He came out of the shopping district, walked past the Nihon University School of Commerce and crossed Setagaya Boulevard, where the traffic was backed up. Just the other day Ryosuke and I had ridden in Momoko to this neighbourhood, to a KFC. It was on our way home from going sunbathing next to the Tama River.

Mr Takashina crossed Setagaya Boulevard and went into the

grounds of a housing complex. I was thinking maybe he lived there, but he just stopped a couple of times to shift the bags from one hand to the other and walked through the grounds and out the other side. The road came out under a high cliff. Since the cliff was topped by a fence, I figured the Setagaya Sports Complex must be up there.

Mr Takashina's house was below the cliff – an old, two-storey single family home, the grounds surrounded by a high concrete-block wall. He opened the rusty metal gate and went inside, without once looking back.

I looked through one of the decorative carved openings in the concrete blocks and saw Mr Takashina, from behind, unlocking the front door. It didn't seem like anyone else was at home. The curtains were closed at all the windows and in the garden there was a layer of withered tulip leaves.

As soon as Mr Takashina went inside, I slipped through a gap in the metal gate and stealthily snuck up to the front door. The nameplate, which said *Tadayoshi and Haruko Takashina,* was slightly lopsided. So his wife, who passed away two years ago, was named Haruko. I straightened the nameplate and slipped back out of the gate and outside. I could sneak into this house any time.

I checked my watch and saw it was almost four. I decided to walk back to Karasuyama by going along the Sengawa River and cutting through Seijo. These days all I seem to do is walk away from somewhere. From the park where I find customers, from hotels where I stay with them, from their apartments, from saunas where I can't sleep well, from Makoto's apartment, where he's been wetting his bed these days because he's overdosing on speed . . . I walk away from all sorts of places, always walking away, but never arriving anywhere.

I remembered Naoki's story of how he ran away from home at fifteen. How when I was working at his company he suspected I was a runaway and told me his own story. Naoki said he'd planned to hitchhike, but took the Chuo Line to Kobuchizawa, then changed to some branch line – which one, he couldn't recall. He can't even remember now which station he finally got off at. Anyway, it was a small, unmanned station, with Mt Yatsugatake rising up before him, and when he left the station he saw a sign for a pension in Kiyosato, so he said, laughing, 'It must have been around there, I guess.'

When he exited the station, the only person getting off there, he found a path through the forest that looked like no one had taken it in years, and with no particular destination in mind he started off down the slope. All sorts of birds called out in the woods.

'A powdery snow started to fall then,' he went on. 'At first just lightly, then soon it was coming down hard. My breath was so thick and white I felt I could grab it with my hand. I'd walked quite a distance from the station, and when it snows in a forest it gets dark very quickly. To tell you the truth, I was getting worried.'

Naoki had apparently left a note behind to his parents about his pointless running away.

'The whole thing was kind of pitiful. I was thinking that maybe I could get home before my dad read the note.'

Right then he spotted a mountain cottage beyond the ever-narrowing path. Trampling down the weeds, Naoki started down an animal trail and walked to the cottage.

'It was less a cottage than a kind of holiday lodge. I knocked many times but nobody came to the door. Yatsugatake is a kind of summer holiday spot, come to think of it. I was about to give up and head back to the station when suddenly, quite suddenly – I'm not sure how to put it, exactly – I heard somebody voice's asking me *Can't you break that window?* It wasn't like I was dying to get inside. Still, that voice was in my head, and it was like I should try getting in, like I *had* to. The rational part of my mind, of course, knew that this cottage was someone else's property and that breaking the window and trespassing was a crime. But I was kind of worked up, having run away from home, and I wanted to break into that mountain cottage, or more strictly into this mountain cottage that was someone else's property . . . Force my way in with my body, like I was physically making the cottage move . . . That's the kind of strange urge that struck me.'

Naoki picked up a stone that was at his feet. The stone was freezing cold, he said. The falling snow had already dyed the leaves on the trees around him white.

'That sound. I can still remember that sound of the stone cracking the glass. From the perspective of the cottage the window I broke was just a small part of it, but the instant that small hole appeared in the glass, it's like – I knew all about the cottage, and the cottage knew all about me.'

Naoki gazed at me with a worried look on his face. 'Do you understand?' he asked.

'No, I don't.' I honestly didn't.

Inside the cottage there were lots of canned goods, still not past their expiry date, smoked hams, and other food. The first night he spent there he was kind of timid, but the next day he grew bolder. He gathered firewood that was underneath the house and on the second night lit a fire in the fireplace. Seated in front of the fireplace, wrapped in a warm blanket, he drank whisky for the first time in his life. After it got light outside, he went for a walk in the forest. A pure white forest bathed in winter sunlight.

'The time I spent there was wonderful. *Wonderful* isn't exactly a word people use much nowadays, I know, but the few days I spent there were really wonderful . . . Wonderful. Yep, seriously wonderful.'

It took me nearly two hours to get back to the apartment in Karasuyama, walking along the Sengawa River, cutting through Seijo.

I opened the front door and was crouching down among the scattered shoes, untying the laces of my trainers, when Koto called out from the living room, 'Hey, Satoru's back!'

'I'm back,' I called out.

Koto said, 'Come here! Hurry up!'

At the same moment Ryosuke clomped out to the entrance. 'Where *were* you?' he scolded me.

'Why're you asking?' I said, a little frightened.

'I've been waiting since yesterday.'

'How come?'

Ryosuke was carrying what looked like a couple of thick study guides. I tugged off my trainers and stepped inside.

'Take a look,' Ryosuke said, looking proud, thrusting the study guides into my chest.

'What are these?'

'Isn't it obvious? They're study guides.'

'Study guides?'

I dodged past him and went into the living room. Two hours of walking and I was looking forward to plopping down on the soft sofa. As soon I entered the living room Koto – dressed in her usual tracksuit – said, 'Thank goodness! He was about to make *me* take the University Entrance Qualifying Exam instead of you, Satoru.'

'Qualifying Exam?'

When I sat down on the sofa my legs suddenly went limp from all the walking I'd been doing since last night.

'Don't you remember what you told me? When we went on that drive to the Tama River?' Ryosuke was still clutching the study guides as he stood there in front of me. I was kind of spacing out and didn't realise he was talking to me until he kicked the sofa.

'Huh? Tama River? Did we go there?'

'Don't you remember? You said you wanted to get a suntan so I took you in Momoko.'

'Oh – that time we picked up KFC on the way back?'

'That's the time. Didn't you say that then?'

'Say what?'

'That you want to go to college.'

Ryosuke began lining up the study guides on top of the table.

'There's no going back now. Ryosuke's totally into it,' Koto said, thrusting a study guide that said *Maths I* on the cover towards me.

'You're kidding. You want me to read this study guide?'

'If you don't, then who will? You're the one who's going to take the test, right?'

'H-hold on a second.'

I hurriedly pulled my hand back from the study guide I was about to take.

It's true that as Ryosuke and I tanned our pale skin on the banks of the Tama River, our conversation somehow drifted to the subject of college.

'What are you going to do after you graduate from college?' I remembered casually asking him.

'I'm going back to my hometown,' he answered calmly.

'Really? But after spending all this time in Tokyo you should get a job here.'

'No way. Three years here has taught me that I'm not cut out for Tokyo. Even now I spend almost all my summer and winter breaks back home.'

'Does everybody know this?'

'Who's everybody?'

'Naoki and the others.'

'No need to tell them.'

'So after you graduate you're moving out of the apartment?'

It was an obvious question, and Ryosuke simply nodded. It was right after this, I think, when I murmured, 'I wonder if my life would change a little if I went to college.' I might have muttered this, but it was just me talking to myself and I never intended to actually go.

Now that I think back on it, though, when I said this Ryosuke, slathering on sunscreen, had this sudden glint in his eyes. A sharp gleam in the eye like he'd spotted his prey.

'Not to worry,' he said. 'I'll put everything I have into tutoring you.'

'It's okay! You don't need to.'

I stealthily pushed the study guides on the table away with my foot so the others wouldn't notice them. As I did, Ryosuke said, 'There's no need to be shy about it.'

'I'm not! But I only graduated from junior high.'

'I know that. That's why they have this kind of test in the first place.'

'I'm telling you, it's impossible. Totally impossible.'

'You won't know that until you try!'

Ryosuke's voice was so intense I flinched. Koto, obviously

enjoying this back and forth, said, teasingly, 'There's no going back now. Your teacher's totally up for this.'

'But I'm telling you, it just won't work.'

I was about to make my escape when Ryosuke grabbed me by the arm.

'It's too late now,' he said, ''cause I made up my mind to do this.'

'You can make up your mind as much as you want, but I'm telling you I can't do it.'

'Well, then what am I supposed to do with all these study guides? I paid money for these.'

'What do I care?'

I tried to brush his arm aside but instead he grabbed me and put me in something close to a sleeper hold – a professional wrestling move. Koto looked at me, choking, gasping for air, and said, breezily, 'You never know unless you try. Why not give it a shot?'

'It's ridiculous, I tell you. I mean, I can't even do fractions.'

'So I'll teach you!'

Ryosuke choked me even harder.

'Hey! That hurts!'

'You'll do it?'

'I told you it's impossible!'

'Then I won't let go.'

Ryosuke applied even more pressure. As he choked me my tongue swelled up.

Koto, flipping through a study guide, laughed. 'I'll help, too,' she said. 'I can't help with your studies, but I'll do things like, you know, make late-night snacks for you, sew good-luck charms onto your clothes, try to avoid unlucky words like *flunk* and *fail*, words like that, and be like a helicopter mum, hovering over you nervously.'

'You'll do it? You'll do it, right?'

As if it were responding to Ryosuke, suddenly the picture on the TV started to go fuzzy again. TVs aren't that expensive these days, but no one here has volunteered to buy a new one. They even compete to see who's best at fixing it.

With Ryosuke's arms still around my neck, I dragged us both over to the TV and, as I'd been taught, pounded its side hard – hard – and then soft.

'Don't worry about the TV. You'll do it, right?'

'Okay, okay! I'll do it. I'll do it, I tell you,' I said, just to get him to stop choking me.

Freed from his grip, I held my throat, coughing like crazy. Koto, seated next to me, said, 'There's like this sense of tension in the air, now that we have a student studying for the entrance exams.' She sounded innocently happy about it.

To tell the truth, I might have stayed here too long. If I go along with playing house any more with them I might find myself not just taking the entrance exam, but working for some top corporation.

NAOKI IHARA (28)

5.1

I had a wisdom tooth out today. Or maybe it wasn't actually pulled out. I can't feel my tongue, so I'm not totally sure. The dentist said, 'The anaesthetic doesn't seem to work well on you, so I gave you twice the usual amount.' He probably had to do that because I didn't get enough sleep the night before.

The dental clinic is on the other side of the station. After they pulled the tooth I got some painkillers at the reception desk, and as I was paying the bill, holding my numb chin, a little boy waiting in the waiting room on the vinyl sofa looked over at me with terror in his eyes. I smiled, trying to put him at ease, but the boy shuddered and quickly looked away. Because of all the anaesthetics maybe my smile was kind of weird-looking.

I left the clinic and walked down the shopping area in front of the station. As I was waiting at the level crossing for a train to pass, the warning bell, which usually bothered me, sounded far away. All my senses were numb.

Back at the apartment, as soon as I opened the door Koto flew out to me from the living room. Behind her stood Mirai, looking pale and hungover, in need of sleep.

'Koto got caught by a salesman. What should she do?'

Mirai was the one asking this, while Koto just stood there, silent, head down.

'Thathsman?' My mouth was still too numb to work well. I tried to say it again and this time drooled. I wanted to hear more and motioned them back into the living room. It was a Saturday morning, but surprisingly Ryosuke was there drilling Satoru on maths problems.

Koto began explaining what had happened. Ryosuke and Satoru took a break from their studying, Mirai was downing an energy drink, and I just sat there, holding my chin.

Yesterday Koto had had a date with Tomohiko Maruyama for the first time in eleven days, she said. After she left the hotel in Ebisu, she was strolling near Dogenzaka when this young guy called out to her. Thinking she'd just kill some time, she followed him to a beauty salon where they made her buy some expensive cosmetics. One after another, customers at other tables were signing agreements to buy the cosmetics, and Koto wound up buying ¥400,000 worth of salon treatments and cosmetics, payable in instalments. When she woke up in the morning she tried to convince herself it was a legitimate purchase, that she hadn't been swindled, but this was too much money for her to keep quiet about. She woke up Mirai, who was groaning about her hangover, and they discussed what she should do. And right then was when I came back from getting my tooth pulled.

'Since you signed the agreement yesterday you should be fine,' I managed to say. 'If you call the Consumer Affairs Bureau and send a notification of cancellation by certified mail, you'll be okay. There's no need to worry.'

Koto's pale face began to get some colour back in it.

'Really?'

'Really. Give the Consumer Affairs Bureau a call.'

I stood up from the sofa. I wanted to check out what the inside of my mouth looked like in the bathroom mirror.

As I stood in front of the mirror the sound came back to me – the *clink* my extracted tooth made when it dropped onto the stainless-steel plate. I didn't actually see the tooth once it was out, but it felt like right now, covered with blood and saliva, it dropped into the sink I was holding on to. Naturally there was no bloody tooth in the sink. Instead there was a long black hair – Koto's, would be my guess – in the shape of a question mark.

I had my mouth open and was staring into the mirror when the door opened behind me.

'I called them and they said I was okay,' Koto's reflection in the mirror said. 'I'm going to get a notification of cancellation now.' Mouth wide open, I looked into the mirror and nodded back.

I carefully rinsed my mouth a few times, watching as the water, mixed with blood and spit, ran down the drain. I left the bathroom and found Ryosuke and Satoru, who should have been studying, gone, and Mirai there, holding her head and groaning. As I stood in front of her she said, 'Did you get it pulled out?'

'Take a look,' I replied, opening wide.

'Does it hurt?'

'I can't feel a thing.'

'Won't it hurt once the anaesthesia wears off?'

'I suppose.'

'You want me to be with you tonight?'

'To do what?'

'Unless you have some drinks, it'll hurt so much you won't be able to sleep.'

I was amazed she could suggest this. I mean, here she was moaning and groaning after drinking too much the night before. Was she being kind? Or did she just want to drink some more herself?

'Where's Ryosuke and the others?' I asked.

'Who knows,' Mirai said. 'Maybe they went with Koto?' She got up from the sofa and, scratching her bum, disappeared into the girls' room.

I don't think Koto acts particularly like an older sister, but Satoru and the others are strangely attached to her.

I went from the living room to the kitchen and gulped down some Volvic. It tasted like watered-down blood. I went into the guys' room, thinking I'd do some laundry, and I saw Ryosuke out on the balcony. So apparently only Satoru went out with Koto. He probably used it as an excuse to get away from the strict regimen Ryosuke had imposed on him.

As I carried the laundry basket out to the balcony I called out to Ryosuke, who was facing away from me. 'What're you doing out here?' He was leaning against the railing, staring down at the Kyukoshu Kaido Boulevard below.

'Hm? Oh, I was just thinking how weird it is,' he said, not turning around.

'What is?'

I went up beside him and looked down at the street below. Nothing looked odd to me. As always cars were moving down the one-lane asphalt road, coming to a halt when the traffic signal directly below us turned red.

'What is?' I asked again.

'See how they never crash into each other?'

I had no idea what he was getting at. I shot him a glance but the answer wasn't exactly written on his face.

'See? They're driving along like that and when the light turns red they all stop, a set distance from each other. Several thousand cars pass by here every day and stop at the light but never hit each other. Don't you find that strange?'

Ryosuke, chin on the railing, continued to gaze down at the street below. 'Yeah, it really is strange,' he repeated. It was sort of strange, I suppose, but nothing to be so impressed about. I didn't reply, walked away from the railing and started doing the laundry. Somebody had left behind a single sock in the washing machine.

I watched the water fill up in the washing machine for a while, then went to the lavatory. I picked up the air-freshener at my feet, started to crush the mushy container in my hands, and when the gel inside was about to spill out I hurriedly stopped. I suddenly remembered that I promised Momochi I'd lend him my suitcase. Next week Momochi and the boss are travelling to the Cannes Film Festival.

Counting the time in college when I worked part-time, I've been with this company for a full eight years. I've never been to the Cannes festival, but to the ones in Berlin and Venice twice each. The Cannes office sent us a pamphlet last month and it looks like there are a lot more interesting films than last year. Momochi and my boss expect David Lynch's new film to win the Palme d'Or, but being more pro-Japan myself, I'm hoping the Japanese master director Shohei Imamura will win an unprecedented third time, despite the fact that his recent works, *The Eel* and *Dr Akagi*, are not his best. The goal in going to festivals, of course, is to purchase distribution rights for films in Japan. But we decided that our budget is such that, unless we get a great deal on a film at Cannes, we're not going to submit any bids.

I left the bathroom and went into the guys' room, opened the wardrobe, and got out my suitcase. I could still see Ryosuke out on the balcony, staring down at the traffic. Next to him the washing machine was chugging away.

Shoving aside Ryosuke's tennis racket and skateboard, I pulled out the suitcase. I think the last time I used it was last year when I went to the AFM film festival in LA. I laid it out in the middle of the room, flipped open the lid and found a Banana Republic shirt inside, with the price tag still attached. It was a woman's shirt, probably a present I bought for Misaki.

Besides the shirt there were some toiletries from the hotel I stayed at, and some books I'd read on the round-trip flight. On the back cover of all three books I'd written down, with a ballpoint pen, the date I'd finished them. In chronological order they were: *Crash*, by J.G. Ballard, Apollinaire's *Lez Onze Mille Verges*, and *The Fall of Macias Guili*, by Natsuki Ikezawa.

I squatted down on the floor and flipped through the pages until the buzzer for the washing machine went off. Our washing machine is the one that Umezaki, who was below me in high school, gave to Ryosuke, who was below him in college. It's the old kind, with separate compartments for washing and wringing out, so you have to take the wash out by hand and put it in the spinner.

The sound of a crash from the street down below came just as I was putting the wash into the spinner. I heard Ryosuke shout and I looked over to see him with his chin resting on the railing. I jumped up and ran over to him. Peering past him, I could see a white saloon that had rammed into a business van.

The bonnet of the saloon was crumpled up a bit and grey smoke was faintly drifting up from the engine. The back window of the van, rammed from behind, had a series of fine cracks running through it.

Ryosuke's face looked just like that of the boy in the waiting room of the dentist's office.

'Th-th-they hit each other.'

'That's 'cause you said that weird thing.'

Naturally what he said and this accident had nothing to do with each other.

The driver of the van was the first to get out, and he seemed unhurt. He walked over to the white saloon and tapped on the window to get the attention of the middle-aged woman driver, who was sitting there looking stunned. She appeared to be resting her chin on the steering wheel, gazing vacantly at the crumpled bonnet, but at the knock on the window she raised her head and suddenly began bowing her head in apology. Unfortunately I couldn't hear them.

'So you saw it?' I said, tapping Ryosuke's shoulder.

'I – I saw the whole thing,' he said excitedly. 'I th-thought traffic was moving normally and they'd stop like they normally do, then there was this loud crash . . . I've seen car accidents before, but never from above like this. I – I reached out my hand to them.'

'Reaching out your hand to do what?'

'I felt like I could stop it!'

The cars behind the white van circled around the car, forming a new stream of traffic. Traffic from the opposite direction started moving *normally* again, as Ryosuke would put it, stopping when the signal was red, moving again when it changed to green, despite the accident.

I couldn't stand there all day, so I went back to my laundry. I was pushing down the inner lid in the spinner when Ryosuke called out again, and I rushed to his side. I followed his finger to the crowd of bystanders around the accident and saw, among them, Koto and Satoru.

'*Heeey!*' Ryosuke yelled out to them. The eyes of the bystanders all moved as one to look up at him, and I unconsciously slipped out of sight behind him. 'Did you see it!?' I could hear Koto yell out clearly. Unconcerned with the stares of the bystanders, Ryosuke yelled back, waving, a proud look on his face, 'I *did*! I *saw* it!'

By the time three policemen had begun their efficient investigation of the accident, the laundry had all been spun dry.

Back in the living room Koto was copying out a clean version of the text the Consumer Affairs Bureau had given her onto the notification of cancellation, and next to her Satoru had a study guide open in front of him and Ryosuke was running him through some trigonometry problems. In the beginning Satoru would find excuses to get away from Ryosuke, but the last few days he's been in the living room, working through the books himself even after Ryosuke goes off to his part-time job.

I hung up the laundry to dry outside and when I went back to the living room, Koto had gone off to the post office, leaving Ryosuke and Satoru across the table from each other, pouting and exchanging sullen looks. 'We did this problem last night!' Ryosuke said. 'No we didn't!' Satoru retorted. I stuck my finger in my mouth to feel my gums. Still no feeling, though there was a faint taste of detergent.

'Okay then. Look at the answer page!' Ryosuke shot back and

headed off to the bathroom. Satoru obediently turned to the answer page.

'It must be hard,' I said, trying to encourage him.

'It's more than that!' he replied, taking it out on me. 'We're doing this day after day.'

'Are you really going to go to college?' I asked, casually flipping through one of the study guides piled up on the table.

'How can I? I don't have that kind of money,' Satoru replied.

'Then what are you studying for?'

'You saw how he is. I can't refuse.' Satoru motioned with his chin towards the bathroom.

'You mean you're studying for Ryosuke?'

'Not exactly.'

Ryosuke emerged from the bathroom, glanced into the guys' room and saw my suitcase. 'You going somewhere, Naoki?' he asked. He'd apparently been so worked up over the accident that when he came in from the balcony he hadn't noticed it the first time.

'I'm lending it to someone at work.'

Satoru, looking through the answer page, asked, 'What are you lending someone from work?'

'Momochi's going to Cannes next week, so I'm lending him my suitcase.'

'To Cannes? By himself?'

'No, the boss is going with him.'

'Won't you need help while they're away? Do you think I can work part-time there again?'

'You want to work for us again? Are you really quitting your job?'

Satoru slowly looked away. 'I haven't actually decided yet . . .' he answered vaguely, tossing the study guide onto the table.

'I'll ask my boss,' I told him, patting him on the shoulder.

Just then Mirai stumbled out of her room and glanced into the guys' room as she made her way to the kitchen.

'You going somewhere, Naoki?' she asked, the same question as Ryosuke. I was about to give the same reply, but before I could Satoru said, 'A person from work is going to Cannes and he's lending it to him.'

'Someone from work?' Mirai asked.

'A person named Momochi,' Satoru said, again answering for me.

5.2

It was a Sunday but in the morning, I went to work anyway. Next week our company is handling the advertising for a Korean film and the lead actress is coming to Japan. There'll be interviews with magazines such as *Esquire* and *Elle Japan* at the Capitol Hotel Tokyu, and we had to readjust the schedule today.

The anaesthesia wore off late last night, and as expected my gums started to ache. I immediately took a couple of aspirins, but Mirai's prediction was spot on – without a drink I wasn't able to sleep – so I waited for her to come back from work and then we went out drinking at a tofu speciality restaurant near the station. Alcohol was, of course, strictly off limits for me, but thanks to the drinks I was able to sleep soundly until morning. But in the morning, even though I took some more aspirins, as I sat in front of my PC my gums started to ache again.

It was just before six p.m. when Misaki called me at the office.

I'd finished work and since, unusually, there was no one else in the office, I'd rented the Taiwanese movie that Misaki had actually recommended, *Dust in the Wind*, from a nearby video store, had watched it on our office's widescreen monitor, and was about ready to go home.

'My mum was here to visit until last night,' Misaki said on the phone. Her mother had brought some gifts for me, and Misaki wanted to meet somewhere for dinner. We each suggested a few restaurants, finally settling on a small Italian restaurant in Yotsuya. Misaki had come by our apartment last week. There's only one reason she wants to see me this often, but listening to her complaints about her boyfriend isn't much fun, I can tell you.

It was after seven when I left the office. I powered down my PC, added more paper to the copier, and was about to leave when a fax came in. I felt like I couldn't ignore it so I went back inside and waited for the sheet to emerge. The fax was a proof of our ad in next month's temp job magazine for a part-timer. The ad was for someone to do office work (including answering the phone), for three or more days per week, at ¥800/hour, with college students welcomed to apply. I recalled how my boss said she might hire a temp to answer the phone, since we were often out of the office. On the back of the fax I scrawled *I have someone in mind. Please keep this pending*, laid it on the boss's desk, and left.

Misaki was already waiting for me when I got to the Italian restaurant. A Ralph Lauren paper bag was on top of the red checked tablecloth. She seemed in a good mood, and even before I got a chance to sit down she started telling me about her mother, who was staying for two or three days in a hotel in Shinjuku. Inside the Ralph Lauren bag was a navy-blue lightweight summer jumper.

'Did your mother say anything?' I asked, holding the jumper up to see how it might fit.

Misaki gave me a knowing look and laughed, 'She did. *Why doesn't he come to see you?* she asked. She said you're a real jerk.'

'Think it'll look good on me?' I asked.

'You don't mind that I already ordered?' she replied.

Occasionally I'll get a phone call from her mother. Of course she knows that Misaki moved out. Her mother will rant on, her usual litany of complaints, for about fifteen minutes, then say, 'Ah! Now I feel better!' and hang up. And just as she's hanging up she'll say, 'Naoki, you probably have a new girlfriend by now?' Misaki's mother's complaints fall into three categories. Complaints about her husband, who runs an accident insurance agency. Complaints about her only daughter living with a boring old fart. And then complaints about worthless me, who'd let her daughter get away.

After we broke up, we would still see each other two or three times a month, so even if we have dinner together there's little new to talk about. I only went out with her for two years, but still I have a feeling we'll be seeing each other in the future. I think she assumes that too. Sometimes she'll say, 'You know, we're pretty efficient. We're making just two years of memories last a lifetime.'

Misaki had ordered pasticho for us, a kind of meat pie. I was carefully cutting into the juicy pie when Misaki asked, 'Is something wrong?' I did feel some pain in my gums as I ate, so I could have laid it to rest by telling her I got a wisdom tooth pulled the day before, but for some reason I couldn't say this, and just said, 'No, I'm feeling okay.' I can't explain it well, even to myself, but I had this kind of vague feeling that I didn't want to easily explain away my attitude by blaming it all on getting a tooth pulled.

We enjoyed a leisurely dessert and it was nine-thirty by the time we left the restaurant. We'd already decided to go somewhere for a drink, but after we cut through an alley and came out onto the main street we found ourselves right at a subway entrance. Somehow the mood was deflated, so we decided instead to go on home and walked down the stairs to the subway.

Misaki was taking the Yurakucho Line so we said goodbye at the ticket machines. She's living now in a high-rise condo her middle-aged boyfriend bought in Harumi. I've never seen the condo, of course, but I can't imagine what sort of place a single guy who, if you round up, is pushing fifty, would possibly buy. Mirai's been there a few times, though, and reported back that, 'That place and ours are like night and day. If that place is Elizabeth Taylor, then ours is Divine.' I can't say I totally followed her explanation.

I arrived at Chidori Karasuyama Station and walked down the shopping district, the fragrance of summer, getting stronger by the day, wafting up on the night wind. I'd gone to work on a weekend so I wasn't wearing a suit, and the breeze wafted in the neck of my polo shirt and gently stroked my chest.

On the way home I stopped by a video rental store. A little place in front of the station, it didn't have Dust in the Wind in stock. I wandered around the store, not really looking for any particular title, and when I came to the corner where videos were lined up according to director, a couple about Satoru's age were looking at a copy of Kubrick's 2001: A Space Odyssey and wondering aloud if it featured any aliens. Finding it funny, I must have been unconsciously staring at them, for the man, noticing me watching them, glared at me with this *What the hell do you want?* kind of look.

As I left there I told them, silently and to myself, *That film doesn't have any aliens, but something much scarier.*

I saw *A Space Odyssey* in a cinema when I was in elementary school – a revival showing, of course. I'd gone to the cinema with my dad many times before then, and compared to my friends watched many more films on TV. I was only a child, but cried at the scene in the Italian film *Sunflower* when Sophia Loren said goodbye to her lover and leapt onto the train, and saw my future self reflected in *Lawrence of Arabia*, which made me feel an oppressive tightness in my chest. But this oppressive feeling was nothing compared to when I saw *A Space Odyssey*. *The Exorcist* hadn't even fazed me, but this was beyond an oppressive feeling – I felt terrified. When I saw that famous last scene where the guy is racing towards eternity, my childish intuition told me there was – well, something in this world that we can never understand, some vastly huge foreign substance, something before which we humans are blown away like so much dust.

As my dad led me by the hand out of the cinema it felt like every single bone in my body had been removed. My body was like a soft lump of flesh, and I couldn't even reply when he asked, 'Did you like it? Was it kind of hard to follow?' The film made me both angry and sad. But was it really me who was feeling angry and sad? I had no idea whose emotions these were, even though they felt so close to me.

In the end I went home without renting a video. When I went inside, the living room was pitch black and nobody was in either the girls' or the guys' room. I hadn't been back to such a dark apartment in a long time, and I reached behind me to shut the front door and stood there for a while in the dark entrance. Standing still in the dark, I started to feel my aching gums again. The deserted apartment was hushed, the only sound the traffic filtering in from outside.

I took off my shoes and walked into the dark living room, and though I wasn't necessarily conscious of it, I could hear my own breathing loud and clear. And then it happened.

'It wasn't you, was it?' Mirai's voice suddenly rose up out of the darkness.

'Woah!' I screamed out. 'Wh-what are you doing? If you need the lights, turn them on!' I yelled this out in a too-loud voice, trying to drown out my pitiful cry, and reached out for the light switch on the wall. The fluorescent light blinked a few times and then came on, revealing a pale-looking Mirai sitting on the floor, her legs formally tucked up underneath her.

'What the heck are you doing?' It was obvious she wasn't just playing a trick, trying to scare me.

'It wasn't you, was it?' she slowly repeated. For some reason she was clutching a video tape.

'What are you talking about?'

'You didn't rummage around in my stuff in my wardrobe, did you?' Mirai stared at a fixed spot on the floor, her gaze never wavering.

'Your stuff? Why would I do that?' With her seated so formally in front of me, I couldn't approach her yet.

'Ryosuke and Koto didn't do it. If you didn't, then Satoru has to be the guilty one . . . I want you to get him out of here! Right now!'

As she screamed this, she threw the video tape against the wall.

The tape hit the wall with a crack and rolled over by my feet. I had no idea what she was talking about.

5.3

I spent the whole day at work sorting through expense receipts. Since we have so few employees I end up doing most of the accounting whenever I have a spare moment. In the afternoon the woman from the tax accountant office came to collect the receipts and told me the same thing she'd said last month: 'Don't try to do it all in one day. Do a little bit each day and then it's simple.'

The boss had apparently already called and stopped the ad for a part-time worker we were set to place in the temp magazine.

'You remember Satoru,' I told her, 'the guy who pasted labels for us the other day?'

'I remember,' she said. 'If part-time work is okay with him, he can start right away.'

After the woman from the accounting office left, the boss and I went out for a late lunch. 'I want to eat something really good for a change,' she said, and we set off for the Sekishintei restaurant in the New Otani Hotel. On the way she started to tell me about an NHK programme she saw recently.

It was a documentary about a young man who was doing Muslim missionary work among the very poor in New York. I wasn't sure how far to trust the boss's memory of the show, but according to her, this young man was talking to a middle-aged black woman, a drug addict, telling her that if she believed, she could make a 'fresh start in life'. A few days later the woman converted to Islam, and as she received a copy of the Koran from him she said, her bloodshot eyes welling up with tears, 'Now I can make a fresh start in life.'

'So what do you think?' the boss asked me.

'I don't know what to say,' I replied.

At Sekishintei there was a choice of two main courses for lunch – Akamatsu snapper or a beef fillet. My boss ordered the snapper so I went with the fillet.

After lunch we left the hotel and were leisurely strolling up Kioizaka slope. At the end of the slope was an embankment with a path along it. In front of us were the sports grounds of Sophia University, and far off we could glimpse the roof of the governmental guesthouse for state visitors. The boss wanted to take a break so I sat down next to her on a bench. The sky was pure blue, the sunlight already holding a hint of summer. As we sat there blankly, kids with matching jerseys, pupils from Kojimachi Junior High, jogged towards us along the path, their pace plodding. Their faces were flushed, their foreheads beaded with sweat in the early summer sun. The dry smell of dust rose up as they jogged by.

'I meant to tell you – I have a girl I want to introduce you to,' the boss suddenly said.

'Um, thanks, but it's okay. I'll find one on my own,' I said, quickly refusing her.

'Are you still moping over the girl you broke up with?' she laughed.

'Isn't moping like this the real thrill of love?'

'Are you serious?'

The boss was turning forty-one this year but somehow she had a boyfriend who was a college student the same age as Ryosuke. One time when we were out drinking, I asked her what type of man she liked. By her tone of voice it was hard to tell if she was serious or joking, but she replied, 'The type of man I go for is like the motto of the Franciscans.' Which, by the way, is *poverty, chastity, and obedience.*

In the evening I attended a meeting of the production team for the pamphlet for a film preview. As always, I had to select the out-of-date design and concept proposed by the director of the company that had made the biggest investment. As we were leaving the conference room I patted Momochi – none of whose designs had been selected – gently on the shoulder and said to him, in an almost desperate tone, 'It's the content of the film that matters! The content of the film!'

Afterwards I didn't return to the office but instead went for a drink by myself at the Halcyon in Aoyama. 'Mirai should be here pretty soon,' the barman told me. I knew that if she got hold of me I'd have to go drinking with her till morning, so I hurriedly got up and was about to leave when Mirai showed up with Shinji, the owner of the imported goods store she worked at. Mirai had clearly already had a few. She spied me at the counter and came right over.

'Did you tell Satoru?' she asked, her breath stinking of alcohol.

'Tell him what?' I said, playing dumb.

'What do you mean, *what*? I asked you to kick him out!'

'But what did he do? Unless I know the reason, I can't just tell him to get out.' I was eating some of the strawberries the owner had put out for me, washing them down with white wine.

'He looked through my belongings! So I want him gone – *now!*' Mirai said.

I hadn't been able to ask Satoru directly what the problem was, since for the last few days he'd stayed away from our place, afraid of Mirai's temper. He apparently slipped back in during the day when Mirai and I were at work, and when Koto asked him what he'd done to upset Mirai so much he'd simply replied, 'I didn't mean any harm. Tell her that if I hurt her feelings, I'm sorry,' but he didn't say anything about the main point – what he'd done in the first place to upset her. My theory was that he'd looked through Mirai's diary, but Koto shot that idea down in no uncertain terms: 'Diary? She doesn't keep one.'

I remembered I had a meeting the next morning so I told her I had to get home and stood up. 'W-wait a sec,' Mirai said, grabbing my arm.

'Then you'd better tell me. What did Satoru do?' I asked again.

'Okay, I get it. I'll tell you. If I tell you, you'll do it, right? You have to kick him out.'

Prefacing her remarks with this, she started to relate the awful thing Satoru had done. In the end I brushed her aside and left the bar. *He recorded* The Pink Panther *over an important video tape of mine*, she'd explained. Not much worse than breaking a nail, if you ask me. Plus this so-called important video was a series of rape scenes from films. Anybody would have wanted to erase that – not just Satoru.

As I exited the bar I could hear Mirai's calling out to me from behind – *Hold on!*

Mirai has the habit, when she's wasted, of falling asleep anywhere she happens to be. One time everybody got up, ready to leave, but we couldn't find Mirai, who'd been carrying on until a few minutes earlier. Figuring she must have left before us, we didn't look for her and started tugging on our coats, which had been piled up on the sofa. And there we found Mirai – asleep under the mound of coats. She was breathing softly and had such a happy smile on her face it made you wonder what sort of dream she was having. It's amazing that she didn't suffocate. Sometimes I feel like asking her what is it that makes her so sad she has to drink so much.

I bought some ice cream at the Baskin Robbins in front of the Chitose Karasuyama Station and went home. Koto was the only one in the living room, Ryosuke was at his part-time job, and was going to stay over at Kiwako's afterwards, and Satoru, still afraid of Mirai, hadn't come back.

Koto was looking a little sad, so I let her choose what kind of ice cream she wanted, then scooped it out for her into a pretty cut-glass bowl, and handed it to her. Koto has a certain presence when it comes to the living room, since she occupies it every single day. Nobody has decided this or anything, but recently, if Koto happens not to be here, nobody sits down in the spot she usually occupies. And Koto's the only one who can tell you right away where the coupons are for pizza, and where the extra boxes of tissues are kept.

Koto was staring, vacantly, not transferring the ice cream in her spoon to her mouth, so I asked her what was wrong. I left the question hanging and went into the guys' room and took off my suit. I was standing in front of the dresser, taking off my tie when I saw Koto, reflected in the mirror, standing in the doorway. Startled, I turned around. Spoon still clutched in her hand, she was staring at my back. I had a bad feeling about this and, trying to pre-empt anything she might say, I said, 'You know, I ran across Mirai today in Halycon, and she was pretty wasted.'

'Naoki? . . . There's something I need to ask you.'

Here we go, I thought, but tried not to let my thoughts show. 'What is it?' I asked. Anything Koto wanted to ask about had to do with Tomohiko Maruyama, I was positive. I'm sorry, but when I come home, tired, that's the last thing I want to talk about.

'What's up? Things aren't going well?' I asked as I took off my shirt, trying not to look her in the eye. Koto, still reflected in the mirror, was looking down.

'I haven't told anybody this yet . . .'

'Um. What is it?'

If you're not telling anybody, then don't tell me, either, okay? I said to myself.

'I tried to be careful, of course . . .'

I could imagine the rest. I tossed my shirt aside and managed to mumble out another *Um*.

'I haven't been able to tell Tomohiko yet . . .'

After I changed into my Adidas tracksuit, I gently nudged her out of the room and into the living room, where we sat down on the sofa.

If, for instance, the baby Koto's carrying were mine, things would be a lot simpler. *Anyway, let's talk about it tomorrow*, I could say, turn off the light and climb into bed. That would itself be an excellent reply. Unfortunately, her baby isn't mine, but that of an actor I've only seen on TV. Plus, though we've lived together these last few months, Koto isn't really one of my close friends. Actually, the sense of distance between us is a difficult thing. I'm not close enough to be hard-hearted with her, but I'm also not far enough removed to pretend to be all warm and kind.

'Doesn't it make sense to first talk with Tomohiko about this?' I said, trying to lay the groundwork for my escape.

'I know, but I just couldn't tell him.'

'Just explain it like you did to me, that was perfect,' I thought. On the table, the ice cream was slowly melting in the bowl.

'Still, you need to talk it over with him.'

'Yeah . . . I know . . . Hey, if you don't want to, that's okay, but could you ask him instead of me?'

The idea had me rattled. Naturally there was this voice, like a basso continuo, droning through me saying *No way, No way,* but – either through timidity or a desire for a quick fix – I found my voice coming out with a pretty half-baked question: 'Huh? Ask him what?'

'What he would do if I were to get pregnant.'

'*If* you were to get pregnant? But you already are, aren't you?'

'True . . . but I think he'd be able to think more calmly if you made it hypothetical – make it *if* I were pregnant, rather than I *am*.'

Was Koto taking Tomohiko for a fool, or was she herself a fool? I licked the chocolate peppermint ice cream without responding. The sweet ice cream melted around my tongue, already numb from the dry wine I'd drunk.

'Have you already been to see a doctor?'

'Not yet. But I did do a home pregnancy test . . . You want to see it?'

'No – I'm good.'

It was pretty clear from her words and attitude that she wasn't planning to keep the baby. But she hesitated to have an abortion without saying anything to Tomohiko, and likewise it would be distressing to face him and hear him say *Get rid of it.* It seemed like she wanted to overcome the problem, and not have any later repercussions, by having a third party like me get involved – and have it come down to a simple *It's okay, right? Right?*

Even after we finished the ice cream Koto didn't budge from

the sofa, and the whole situation was feeling so stifling I couldn't even get up to use the loo. Finally – wanting to escape this unbearable moment – I said, 'Okay. I'll do it. I'll talk with Tomohiko. But I should do it soon. The baby won't wait.' I already regretted speaking so agreeably about it, afraid she would start consulting me about one thing after another.

'I – I suppose so,' Koto said, standing up and trotting into the girls' room. She emerged clutching a notebook that apparently had Tomohiko's schedule in it.

'Let's see – if it's next week, how about Tuesday night? Or Thursday morning?'

Koto's tone was so oddly cheery, in no way the voice of someone deciding which day to announce she was getting an abortion.

The last few years it seems like things always go in a different direction from the way I think they will. What I mean is, the things that I do entirely for my own benefit are often misinterpreted by those around me as being done out of concern for others. One example would be when Misaki said she'd bring Mirai to live with us, I agreed simply for the selfish reason that I thought that if Mirai joined us, Misaki and I wouldn't have our usual fights every night. Still, Misaki and Mirai, and even the owner of Halycon, praised me for being so generous and open-minded. The same thing happened when Ryosuke was brought in. When Umezaki, who was below me at high school, said there was a younger guy at his college who was disappointed in love and might kill himself, I did tell him, 'In that case, you'd better bring him on over.' But again this was only out of a kind of sordid spite, since I was envious of Misaki and Mirai, who were enjoying themselves so much and ignoring me, and I figured I could force them to have to deal with a guy on the verge of suicide. Ryosuke was supposedly so depressed that he was near suicidal, but once he started living here, he perked up, and later Umezaki said to me, with obvious respect, that he 'knew I could do it'. And letting Koto live with us came about because, after Misaki moved out, the place had turned into a pigsty. If Koto didn't like cleaning as much as she did, who would ever want to live with her – no matter how pretty she is – since all she does is sit there in the living room all day long, waiting for a guy to call.

So even though I'd only done things that would benefit me, whenever any of them – be it Koto, Ryosuke, Mirai, or Satoru – have a problem they always come to me for advice, like it's the most natural thing in the world. Never once have I really been kind and considered the other person's situation, but still they come to me, like Koto's asking my advice this evening. Even so, perhaps through some twisted part of their personalities, they view this detachment as consideration, and I find my stock, despite my unwillingness, rising in their eyes.

Before I knew it, my lack of genuine concern led them to treat me like some great elder brother figure. If they're satisfied with selfish consideration like this, then how does the rest of the world treat them? The thought has me worried. No – I'd better stop thinking that way, otherwise they'll just ask me to help with something else.

5·4

For the first time in a long while, I jogged every single day for a week. It feels much more refreshing to run in the morning, when the air's crisp, rather than after I come back from work. Ryosuke jogged with me for two days, but on the third morning when I asked him to join me, he didn't even try to crawl out of bed. When I'm in good shape and feel a sort of pleasant exhaustion, strangely enough it makes me long for physical contact. On Sunday, by coincidence, Misaki came to stay over. She had on a long skirt of thin, flower-patterned material, and a T-shirt that made her breasts stand out. This is the outfit of hers I like the best of all. As she was enjoying the yokan sweets she'd bought she said, 'Sometimes don't you want to do it in a weird place?'

'Weird place? What do you mean? Like in Ryosuke's bed?' I kidded her.

'Are you kidding? With his slobber all over the covers?'

'Okay, so where, then?'

We were talking this over for a while when Koto came back from a rare trip outside the apartment.

Three days before, I'd met Tomohiko Maruyama in a small coffee shop in Ebisu. He wore a hat pulled down low, but even so three of the waitresses in the shop pestered him for his autograph. He looked a lot younger in person than on TV. I figured TV personalities like him must be pretty disagreeable people, and I didn't want things to get too complicated, plus I was sure he had a tight schedule, so I went right ahead and told him what was going on.

'I see,' he said in quiet voice, adding, 'I need a little time to think about it.'

I was almost about to tell him that *Koto isn't planning to keep the baby*, but seeing how terribly earnest he was, I couldn't very well tell him *Don't you think Koto would be relieved if you told her to get rid of it?*

'I'll get in touch with her within a week,' he said and left the coffee shop. If he did tell her to keep the baby, I thought worriedly,

I wonder what she'd do? Probably in a couple of days Koto would get the fateful call.

As Koto was getting a bottle of Volvic out of the fridge I asked her, 'Where did you go?'

'To vote in the election,' she said, as if it were nothing.

'To vote? You mean you transferred your registration to here?'

'No, not yet. Mirai said she couldn't go, so I went to vote for her,' Koto said and disappeared into the girls' room. No matter how tired she might be from waiting for Tomohiko to call, she didn't seem to have an inkling of the fact that she'd just committed a serious crime.

Right then, next to me, Misaki called out, 'Ah! I've got it! I know a great weird place!'

Where Misaki took me was a neighbourhood elementary school that was also being used for voting.

'Here?'

I started to edge backwards. 'It's okay. If we sneak in quietly,' Misaki said, full of confidence. She gave me a nudge and I stepped over the off-limits rope and trespassed onto the school grounds. As she'd said, once we were inside, nobody was going to find us. We went down the hallway, keeping our heads low, and went up the stairs to the second floor. The first classroom we came to was a fourth-grade classroom, Class No. 1, and I carefully slid open the door so as not to make any sound. In the hushed classroom the beige curtains were closed and the afternoon sunlight was faintly shining in. I hadn't seen elementary school desks and chairs for a long time and they looked like toys. Misaki and I sat down next to each other in the tiny chairs.

'What kind of child were you in elementary school?' she asked.

'Just an ordinary kid,' I replied. I stuck my hand inside the desk and came out with a slice of rock-hard bread. Misaki was leafing through a music textbook.

I went over and sat down in the seat in front of her, twisted around and kissed her.

'This is really turning me on,' she said. She was right – the excitement was getting to me, too.

We couldn't bring ourselves to strip completely naked, but when I saw her white breasts spill out when she pulled up her T-shirt it was so sexy and obscene I wanted to trample on them. She pulled her lips from mine and suddenly asked, 'Do you still love me?'

I thought it over for a moment, then replied, 'That's a bit of a burden to lay on me don't you think? But I guess I do still love you.'

She laughed through her nose, and muttered, 'You haven't changed at all.'

'What do you mean, I haven't changed at all?'

'It means what it means,' Misaki said, readjusting her bra. Just then we heard a sound out in the hallway and we looked at each other and held our breath. The sound of the footsteps proceeded at a steady pace, apparently going down the stairs.

'Did you hear about Mirai?' she asked.

'What about her?'

'I don't know if she's serious, but she said she's going to Hawaii.'

'Hawaii? With who?'

'Not on a trip, but to move there.'

'To *move* there?'

'Yeah, but you know her. I don't know how much to believe. She was at some bar drinking with Satoru and the others and she met the president of a confectionary company from Kobe. Apparently they have a company holiday place in Oahu and they were talking about having her be the manager.'

'What do you mean, manager?'

'I don't know. But she showed me pictures of the place and it's a pretty high-end condo.'

'But that was just something they talked about over drinks, right?'

'I can't really say.'

As she said this, I stood up from the tiny chair and went over to check out the hallway. I looked down the long hallway but there didn't seem to be anybody walking there. It felt like if I listened carefully I could make out the echo of children's laughter.

That night Misaki and I went out for dinner, just the two of us. We invited Koto, in the living room as always, but she turned us down flat, saying that at ten there was a drama on TV that Tomohiko was in. Mirai wasn't back yet from work, Ryosuke was at his part-time job, and as usual, we hadn't heard from Satoru.

We had dinner at a new place near the station that specialised in beef tongue, then had some wine at a bar run by a Frenchman. It was after ten when we got back home, a bit tipsy, and when we went into the living room Tomohiko Maruyama himself was sitting there, a serious look on his face. 'Ah! Ah!' Misaki exclaimed, pointing back and forth – first at the real-life Tomohiko, then at him on the TV screen, where he was running underneath some cherry trees.

Sensing the atmosphere in the room I tugged Misaki by the hand and we slinked off to the guys' room. 'Wow – Koto really *is* dating Tomohiko Maruyama,' Misaki said blithely, and stuck her ear against the door. 'Knock it off,' I said, roughly pulling her away by the arm.

For a while all we could hear from the living room was the TV. From what I knew of last week's episode, the young guy that Tomohiko was playing had started to live in an old apartment together with Ryo Ekura, who was still heartbroken from having her friend steal her boyfriend away from her. *I can't stand holding you while I know you're thinking of him* – this corny line in his voice came out of the TV speakers, filtered out through the living room where the actual person who spoke it was, and reached the guys' room.

'This feels kind of weird,' Misaki said.

'What does?'

'It's like he's actually there saying that,' she laughed. And she was right. Who needs the TV? I thought.

We could hear what Koto and the real Tomohiko were saying only when the programme went to an ad break. Despite my warning, Misaki had her ear plastered against the door.

To summarise the conversation in the living room: Koto said she didn't want to 'cause him any trouble' so she didn't want to have the baby, to which Tomohiko tried to persuade her that 'No, it's not causing any trouble. I'm sure things will work out.' This was his way of putting on a good face – what they were really desperately searching for was a credible reason to choose an abortion. If the popular actor was telling her to 'Get rid of it!' while the young fan was insisting that he 'Let me have it!' you could pretty much figure out how things would work out, but here, with the opposite happening – the popular actor telling her to keep it while the young fan wants the abortion – it's hard to know how the story will end.

Misaki, ear pressed against the door, laughed. 'It's like an anti-melodrama. Soap operas in Spain, though, sometimes play out

like this.' I knew nothing about Spanish soap operas – instead what
came to mind was Almodóvar's film *What Have I Done to Deserve
This?* I recalled how in an interview in a magazine the director
said, 'A person's face filled with joy and one twisted in agony are
identical . . . I made this movie as if the Franco regime never
existed.'

When the TV drama finished Tomohiko said, 'Nice seeing
you,' to me and Misaki, and left. His manager was apparently
waiting for him. At least as far as what we heard through the
door, the two of them hadn't resolved their problem.

I didn't want to go out to the living room and hear Koto rehash
the whole conversation, so I stayed in the guys' room. Misaki went
instead, and prefacing her remarks with the comment that 'I didn't
intend to overhear anything,' she said, in a rather severe tone,
'You'd better make a decision soon. The baby won't wait for you.'
Koto was silent and Misaki went on: 'Tomohiko's acting nice to
you, so you're trying to make it last as long as possible, right?' The
sort of *coup de grâce* comment you'd only find between two women,
something I can't imagine me ever saying.

Misaki went home that night without staying over. Mirai came
back, drunk, after two a.m. She came into the guys' room and
though I knew she turned on the light I pretended to still be
asleep. But she shook me so hard I finally gave in. 'What d'ya
want?' I said, blinking my eyes in the white fluorescent light.

'I was at Brodsky, in Shimokita, drinking with Ryosuke,' Mirai
said.

I checked below my bed and sure enough Ryosuke's futon was
still neatly folded up.

'He was with Kiwako. They seem pretty tight.'

'Um,' was all I said.

'They said Satoru's left. They said he took his belongings and left.'

Did Satoru even have any belongings? I wondered.

'Where do you think he's gonna sleep tonight?'

'Maybe at a friend's place?' I replied kind of bluntly and turned my face to the wall. Oblivious, Mirai went on talking.

'Once Satoru took me to Hibiya Park. It was the middle of the night and we snuck into an outdoor concert hall. He sleeps there when he doesn't have anywhere else to stay. There were these long benches around the stage and we lay down on them. They were awfully cold. Those benches will make your back hurt they're so cold at night. It was the middle of Tokyo but it was quiet – just the sounds of cars far away – and it made me feel kind of lonely . . . He's only eighteen, you know. Yet he's slept at that kind of place many times.'

As I listened to her from behind me, I suddenly remembered that I hadn't told Satoru about the part-time job I had for him. Before, when he was helping paste the labels for the invites to the film preview and I told him he could go home, he said he wanted to help out a little more. I recalled how he looked trying, and messing up a few times, to use the copy machine.

'Are you sleepy?' Mirai sounded a little lonely.

'No, not really,' I replied.

'Have you seen Satoru's face when he's asleep on the sofa? He's still just a child . . . Still a child, yet he doesn't have any place to live, and he sleeps on a bench in a park.'

I rolled over and found Mirai's face right next to me. We gazed at each other, and an odd silence came over us.

'Naoki, you think I'm some lesbian who hates guys, right?'

'Huh? Where did that come from?'

'No need to be so afraid . . . Oh, did you think I was going to kiss you?'

Her breath reeked of vodka.

'You won't know unless you try, right? You remember that fortune teller next door, how he said you're looking for a change? Maybe tomorrow something will change.'

'It's okay. I don't need to force things.'

'And here I was trying to help you.' With this she switched off the fluorescent light and left the room.

If you break out of this world you'll find this world again, only one size larger . . . I'm pretty sure this is what the fortune teller had said.

5·5

Koto phoned me at the office. 'Satoru just called me a while ago and I told him to call you there about the job. Did he call?' She sounded strangely happy.

'No, not yet,' I answered curtly, since I was busy.

'I see. So you haven't asked him yet?'

'Asked him what?'

'Where he's staying now.'

With my boss and Momochi on a business trip to Cannes, I was spending the whole day answering the phone. Wanting to get off, I asked her, kind of brusquely, 'So where's he sleeping?' To which Koto, sounding a little self-important, laughed, 'Satoru's sleeping every night in Momoko.'

'Not at a friend's place?'

'He was in the beginning. But his friend got arrested for marijuana possession.'

Just then another phone rang. 'Sorry,' I said, about to hang up.

Koto said, 'Why don't you stop by the car park tonight and bring Satoru back?'

'Okay,' I said, 'I'll do that,' and I hung up. But right after that, I answered a call from an illustrator and while we discussed the details of colour selection I completely forgot what I'd promised to do.

After this the phone rang incessantly. Questions from the media about the preview showing, a publisher asking for colour positive film, a magazine wanting to do a report, proofs from the printer that needed checking. As I answered all four office phones my hand and tone of voice both grew mechanical, and I felt an odd uplifting feeling surge through me. The moment I hung up one phone another would start ringing, like it was lying in wait. If I didn't reach out for it, the comical ringing would just continue. Soon another phone would start up ringing, the two bells like musical sound. I let out a deep breath and from the pit of my stomach laughter rose up. Right then a shudder ran up my spine. I wasn't at Cannes making a film deal, and I wasn't at some planning session giving a presentation. I was simply in a tiny, deserted office, trying to keep up with all the phone calls. Even so, the situation gave me a certain sense of joy, which sent a chill through me.

The phone kept on ringing. I faced the phone and murmured, 'I'm fed up.' My voice didn't sound real. Once again, in a louder voice, I yelled out, 'I'm fed up!' As it echoed in the cramped office, though, to me it sounded more like I'd shouted out *I'm happy!*

I left work early for the first time in a long while, and when I got home Ryosuke and Koto were in the living room, side by side, watching TV together. I was sure it was some love drama again, but it was actually an NHK documentary detailing how the Matsushita Corporation, which had purchased MCA, had withdrawn from the Hollywood entertainment business. I ended up sitting down with them and watching it to the end.

The programme ended and I was heading to the guys' room to change when I heard Koto behind me say, 'I'm going to the hospital next Tuesday.'

I answered with a reflexive 'Um', and headed into my bedroom. Then I came to a halt. 'The hospital?' I said, and whirled around. 'So you're going to get rid of it?'

Koto, still watching TV, gave a deep nod.

'Are you sure you're okay with that?' I asked the back of her head.

'Yeah. Thanks,' she replied. What she was thanking me for I had no idea. But maybe there was no need for me to poke my nose into it any further. I went into the guys' room without saying anything more, and took off my suit. As I changed into a jersey I asked myself if I would act the same way if Koto were my kid sister. That's stupid, I reconsidered. She's not my sister.

The fluorescent light in the bedroom was on the blink. In the flickering white light, my naked upper body was reflected in the sliding glass door. As the light flickered, my image would appear clearly, then disappear, on and off. As I stared at this succession of images, a vague, pale shadow that seemed right in between remained in my field of vision. Suddenly I thought of the foetus inside Koto's belly. And how she had nodded without looking in my direction.

I switched off the annoying, flickering light, and the room, now pitch black, seemed to be swallowed up in the night outside.

After standing there for some time, I realised there was light from the living room at my feet. It was Koto, looking through the slightly ajar door, an embarrassed look on her face as she gazed at me standing there vacantly in the middle of the dark room. Caught unaware, I hurriedly explained: 'The fluorescent light's not working well,' pulling the cord for the light. When Koto saw how the light flickered, she seemed relieved.

As I tied the belt on my jersey I asked her what she wanted. It turned out Koto and Ryosuke were going to rent a video and wondered if I had any recommendations for new films.

'What are you doing? Let's go,' Ryosuke shouted from the front door.

'Sorry,' I said, 'I can't think of any,' and I guided Koto out the door and went into the living room.

After they'd left for the video store, I switched off the TV they'd left on and sat down on the sofa. Under my bum I found Ryosuke's keyring, and I picked it up. It was a black leather holder with five keys. One key was for the apartment, another was most likely for Momoko, but I wasn't sure about the remaining three. One was maybe for Kiwako's apartment, and another for his parents' home. But what the fifth key was for I had no clue. I tossed the keyring onto the table and the five keys made a pleasant clatter.

Since I'd turned off the TV it was so quiet I could hear the second hand on the wall clock. I shifted my weight and the fake leather of the sofa creaked. The living room was almost always occupied, and I hadn't been alone in it like this for quite some time. Restless, I stood up and turned on the TV. And I continued over to the girls' room, which I hadn't been in recently, and went in. Mirai had moved the bed to a slightly different spot from where Misaki used to have it. I turned on the light and made a half-circuit of the bed. A futon, the one Koto must sleep in, was neatly folded up on the floor, with a batik cover over it. Three cardboard boxes were lined up against the wall, with what appeared to be her clothes inside. This was all she had. I happened to nudge one of the boxes with my foot and saw invoices for a parcel delivery service stuck between them. I pulled the invoices out and saw they were already all filled in, in pen. The receiver's address was Koto's parents' address. *From: Kotomi Okochi, Tokyo. To: Kotomi Okochi, Hiroshima.* Packages sent from her to herself. There were three invoices, one for each of the three boxes that contained Koto's belongings.

Oddly, I felt nothing. Koto may be leaving here. She might not be here any more. These were my thoughts, but no emotion welled up as a result. Actually, I may have been thinking the same thing from the time she first moved in. It was like I was saying *Let's live together from today* and *Okay, see you. Bye!* at one and the same instant . . . Like from the moment things began, we'd reached the end. Maybe from the day Koto first came here she had already left. Maybe these last few months I'd been enjoying living not with the Koto who would someday leave, but with the after-image of the Koto who had already left.

I wasn't counting on Koto to be thoughtful enough to buy a new fluorescent light bulb, so I went out to buy one. The exact moment I opened the front door the fortune teller from 402 next door emerged from his place, a bin bag in each hand. I'd seen him several times but had never spoken to him. Since we were looking right at each other, I said good evening but the fortune teller bluntly turned away. I'm not sure why, but I apologised.

From behind his closed front door I could hear cats mewing.

Not just one, but five or six cats irritably meowing and scratching at the door with their claws.

I didn't feel like getting in the same lift as him, so I took the stairs down to the ground floor, but as luck would have it right when I arrived the lift door opened and again we came face to face. This time I looked away first. In the corner of my eye I sensed him giving a reluctant bow, but I had broken eye contact so openly I couldn't very well face him again.

I left the building, wove my way through the cars as I crossed the street, and went into the convenience store across the way. I bought two energy-saving fluorescent bulbs and a bunch of slightly black bananas. I left the store and was about to cross the street again when I spotted a man in a suit coming down the emergency stairs next to the convenience store. The first and second floors of the convenience store building were offices of a life insurance company, the third floor was an acupuncture clinic, while the owner of the building occupied the fourth floor. Out of pure curiosity, I decided to go up the emergency stairs the man had come down.

When I got to the landing between the third and fourth floors, our own apartment building across the street was completely exposed to view. Our apartment was long and narrow, so the windows for all three rooms – the guys' room, the living room, and the girls' room – faced the street. The lights were on in all the rooms, with the florescent light in the guys' room, as always, flickering. The TV in the living room was still on. The girls' room was a bit dim, but with the curtains open I could clearly see Mirai's illustrations hanging on the wall.

I put the plastic bag with the two fluorescent bulbs and bunch of bananas down at my feet, rested my chin on the metal railing, and gazed at our apartment. No one was in any of the rooms. It felt strange to be viewing the rooms from the outside like this. Not because no one was there, but it was strange to think that we actually lived inside there. I wanted to see somebody inside those three empty rooms. If I waited a while, Koto and Ryosuke should be coming back from the video store.

For some reason, I suddenly thought of Satoru. One time when we went to the ramen place in front of the station, Satoru was holding a plate of fried rice and as he shovelled it in he said, 'I have a favour to ask.' I was only sort of half listening.

'I have this friend named Makoto, and I was wondering if it'd be okay if he comes to live with us.'

According to Satoru, he'd already talked this over with Koto, and had asked Ryosuke and Mirai, and all three of them were against it. And he wanted me to ask them again. I was eating the ramen as he spoke, and I sipped down the last bit of soup right as he finished. I put the bowl down and looked up and saw Satoru staring at me. Almost unconsciously I said, 'Aren't you kind of jumping to conclusions?' For a second his face went pale. 'Well – what I mean is,' I hurriedly added, 'you don't have any place to stay, right?'

'Yeah, that's true,' he replied, and fell silent.

I remembered all this as I stood there on the landing of the emergency stairs, vaguely watching our empty apartment across the street.

Ryosuke and Koto didn't seem to be coming back, no matter how long I waited, and I was about to give up and go home when a navy blue BMW pulled up outside our building. It was Misaki who emerged from the passenger side and I leaned over the railing and was about to call out to her, but she went around to the driver's side and was trying to pull this guy I'd never seen before out of the car against his will. The guy who got out was a drab, middle-aged man, who I figured must be Tanitsu, Misaki's boyfriend. Dragging the reluctant man along, Misaki went inside the entrance. I thought of following them, but decided to stay out and watch.

Misaki soon appeared in the living room. Her mouth was moving a little, maybe calling out to the man, who was still at the front door. Misaki opened the door to the guys' room. She disappeared from sight for a second, then reappeared under the flickering fluorescent light. The man still hadn't made an appearance. Misaki switched off the flickering light. The three lit-up rooms became two, and she exited the guys' room, cut through the living room and went into the girls' room. I waved to her, but she wasn't looking outside.

This was when the man came inside. He nervously looked around and motioned to Misaki to come, probably telling her they should leave. She came back into the living room and shrugged and held both hands out wide, the way foreigners do. It looked like a poorly performed pantomime. I could see the man's face from the front. Nothing special. Misaki dragged him into the girls' room and pointed to where her bed used to be, no doubt telling him *This is where I used to live.* And that's when it happened. The man was scanning all of Mirai's illustrations up on the wall, when his eyes pierced through the window and ran smack into mine. It felt like our eyes both wavered for an instant. I didn't look away, and he moved his gaze away from me and back to the walls of the room, in an entirely natural way, as if he'd never seen me. He took Misaki's hand and pulled her back to the living room.

After this they sat on the sofa for about ten minutes. I could see the guy get up a few times, tugging at Misaki's arm. The rest of the time it was just their heads as they faced each other on the sofa.

As I watched their stationary heads, a strange doubt welled up in me. I was vaguely thinking how Misaki lives now in a high-rise condo in Kiyomi and the strange doubt that suddenly hit me was this: not just Misaki, but everyone else who lives in our apartment might actually be living somewhere else . . . Just like Misaki lives in the high-rise condo in Kiyomi, maybe all of them – Mirai, Koto, Ryosuke, and Satoru – all have their own places somewhere else? Which means that the only one who actually lives in this apartment I was looking at is me. The whole idea is impossible, but somehow this strange fantasy threw me.

I remember how, back when Misaki and I were living together, before Mirai moved in, and things weren't going too well with us, Misaki said this:

'It's just the two of us living here, you and me. But sometimes it feels like there's someone else here. I can't explain it well, but it's like there's this monster that you and I have created.'

She didn't go on to say, 'And it's because of that that we've grown hostile to each other.' She was merely saying that, like it or not, when people come together they give birth to that sort of thing.

Misaki and her boyfriend left before Ryosuke and Koto came back. I went down the stairs when they came down, and from the landing between the first and second floor, watched them as they exited the building. Under the street light I could see Tanitsu's face more clearly this time. Like I thought before, he was nothing special.

I waited until they'd driven away before crossing the street. I went into our apartment, opened the living-room window, and directly across was the landing where I'd been standing. Right below the railing was the plastic bag with the two fluorescent lights and the bunch of bananas. I clucked my tongue, and kicked the side of the sofa Misaki and her boyfriend had been sitting on. The plywood inside broke with a loud crack. I kicked it again and my toes sunk deep inside the hole I'd made.

The smell of rain came in from the window. I went out on the balcony and looked up at the sky, but there were no rain clouds, just the pale moon. I suddenly recalled how the fortune teller next door only read fortunes around the time of a new moon or a full moon. The moist night air stroked my cheeks, blowing in the sleeves of my T-shirt and tickling my underarms. When I turned around, the brand new fluorescent lights I'd put in were dazzlingly bright.

I went back inside, changed into my jogging gear and went back out to the living room. Ryosuke and Koto were still out, maybe stopping at a karaoke place after the video store. Mirai wasn't back yet, probably out drinking somewhere. I glanced at the wall clock, and it was already eleven.

As I was tying my laces up tight at the front door, I thought about where I should run. Going east down Kyukoshu Kaido Boulevard, then over Kanpachi to Bashikoen would be good, and I felt I had more than enough energy to head north, go under the overpass for the Metro Expressway and make it all the way to Inokashira Park.

I was doing a few warm-up leaps in the entrance when I heard, outside the door, Ryosuke and Koto laughing. I opened the door and saw them walking down the hallway towards me. Their eyes both went to my feet and for some reason for a second they both looked annoyed.

'You guys really took your time,' I said.

'You're going jogging?' Koto said. 'We had a parfait on the way back,' Ryosuke said, their voices overlapped. Ryosuke was holding a bag from the video store.

'So what did you get?' I asked.

'It's a secret,' Ryosuke replied.

'And we were hoping so much to watch it with you,' Koto said slyly.

'I can't, I'm going running,' I said.

'I guess not, then.'

Koto and Ryosuke came in and I went out the door, almost shoved out the narrow entrance. 'So what did you end up renting?' I asked again.

As she removed her shoes Koto laughed. 'Porn.'

'Don't look at me!' Ryosuke protested. 'She's the one who wanted to rent it.'

I shut the door and proceeded down the corridor. I got in the lift and when I did some deep knee bends, the floor bowed downwards.

At the entrance to the building I did some more warm-up exercises. Through my headphones I could hear Maria Callas – the aria 'La mamma morta' from *Andrea Chénier*. I stretched out my Achilles tendons, pushed rewind on the tape, took a deep breath, and set off.

I left the entrance and came out on Kyukoshu Kaido Boulevard. I hadn't decided which route to take, but my feet turned left. I ran down the white line on the pavement between the pedestrian path and the street. Whenever there was an electric pole in the way, the straight white line twisted out towards the road, and then the slightly bulging line went back to the way it had been. As I swerved around a couple standing there talking, and an illegally parked car, Maria Callas's voice swelled up again. It felt good to be running down the streets like this at night, listening to this aria, to the plea for mercy. It was like I was escaping the world, and my legs felt stronger for it. I timed my breathing with my strides. My feet seemed to glide across the ground. Whenever I swerved out into the street a little, headlights would draw near from behind. The car would pass by with inches to spare. One car after another passed me. The world I should be escaping from was still pulling ahead of me. I turned left at Matsuba Boulevard. Cross this narrow street and you come out on Route 20.

As I ran, I noticed all kinds of unusual things. A crack in the pavement. A guard rail bent by an accident, a throwaway ad sign, folded over, a flickering street light, a brilliant hydrangea sticking out between a concrete block wall.

I came out on Route 20. At the intersection the green light for pedestrians was flashing. I decided to go for broke and raced across the broad road, which has three lanes on each side. The headlights of the stopped cars seemed to sear my cheeks. The sweat waiting just under my skin now gushed out my pores. Just when I got to the median, the light turned red. I sped up even more and raced across the rest of the brightly lit crossing. The instant my left foot reached the far side a car whizzed by, like the bridge I'd just crossed had collapsed behind me.

I passed the young couple who had been leisurely crossing ahead of me and headed north along Matsuba Boulevard. The sound from my Walkman cut out for a second and the music switched from 'Habanera' to 'Je veux vivre dans ce reve'. Just for a moment, at the pause between songs I could hear the hard sound of my feet as they hit the pavement. When the music started up again, though, the asphalt felt soft, like I was running down a rotting, mushy old linoleum floor. Like it wasn't the earth, but skin covering the earth.

A cavernous darkness spread out before me. At Takaido the Metro Expressway branches off from Route 20, and the elevated bridges on the motorway rise up in the night sky as if about to crush the streets below. As I ran underneath the elevated bridges, I turned left and ran alongside the concrete bridge. At the time of the 1995 Kobe earthquake on TV I saw the same sort of bridge toppled over. I suddenly looked up. Even now, hundreds of cars were silently gliding along that bridge.

No one else was on the deserted, dark street underneath the bridge, just the crossing light changing from green to red. There was a fence between the thick pillars, and the bare concrete walls shone palely in the street lights. Graffiti was sprayed on the wall in black paint. I couldn't make out what was drawn there, but it was kind of amateurish. Once before when I was running here, there was a group of skateboarders yelling in sort of weird, angry voices. But tonight I didn't see them.

I jogged on, not breaking stride. I suddenly smelled dirt, and just then raindrops plopped down on my cheeks. Before I even noticed it, rain clouds had covered the sky, the colour you'd get if you mixed every colour of paint together. The rain spattered down on my bare arms and ears. The street lights lit up the rain-drops as if they were a cloud of beetles. I suddenly recalled that the car park where Ryosuke parked his car was just up the street. Satoru might be there, I thought.

Every time I ran under the street lights, my dark shadow formed at my feet. With each step the shadow stretched out ahead of me, and as the next street light approached it faded away. When I turned around and ran backwards, a different shadow formed at my feet and trailed away behind me.

For Setagaya, there were still a lot of farm fields around. The car park that Ryosuke rented a space from was in the middle of one of these fields. I could feel the gravel in the car park against my feet. My ears, though, were still full of the voice of Maria Callas.

Ryosuke's car was all by itself in one corner of the spacious car park. As I entered the car park I gradually slowed down and, catching my breath, started walking. It was pitch dark. As I got near the car, I could see the raindrops flowing down the windscreen. I leaned up against the driver's side window and peered inside. In the back seat there was a rumpled blanket and pillow and a few manga books. The window clouded up with my breath. The body of the car felt a bit warm to the touch. Raindrops slid down the back of my neck and slowly down my back and made me shiver.

I decided I should go back home before it started raining hard. I left the car and started slowly jogging back out of the car park. The smell of dirt got even stronger. The rain didn't wait. Even over Callas's powerful voice I could hear the sound of it as it struck the ground. My shoulders got wet and my T-shirt slowly grew heavy. The rain ran down my hair and forehead and got in my eyes, and the light of a far-off traffic signal looked blurry.

By the time I got back to the elevated bridge over the motorway, my T-shirt was plastered against my chest and stomach. Rain and sweat were slowly soaking into the elastic band of my shorts. I tried to wipe my wet face but my palm was soaked. I crossed under the elevated bridge and stopped at the median, thinking I'd look for somewhere to get out of the rain. I leaned my hand against the rusty fence and bent over to catch my breath. A mix of sweat and rain – it was hard to tell one from the other – dripped down to my feet, wetting a chunk of concrete that lay there. A rusty reinforcing bar stuck out of the concrete. From far away a car was getting nearer. Its headlights illuminated the graffiti on the pillars of the bridge, and it sent up a splash as it drove past me and away.

It was right then that I heard a faint sound of somebody's footsteps. It was between songs and the only thing I could hear was my ragged breathing. I looked up and saw a woman with a red umbrella slowly crossing towards me. The woman didn't seem to have noticed me. Her feet, in white sandals, looked muddy. I picked up the chunk of concrete and hid behind a pillar. Having run so hard, my stomach cramped up and I felt nauseous. The woman's face was hidden behind the red umbrella and I couldn't see it. When I leapt out from behind the pillar I caught a glimpse of her mouth. For some reason she seemed to be smiling.

I don't remember exactly what I did next. When I realised what I was doing, I had my hand clamped over her mouth and had shoved her against the rusty fence. I couldn't hear her scream. When I drove the chunk of concrete against her face, all I felt was it smashing against her, the chunk of concrete sinking in her soft face. I swung my hand up once more. The concrete chunk came right out of her face. Something black oozed out of the woman's open mouth, like there was one more row of teeth between the upper and lower ones. The woman's eyes were crossed. I brought the concrete back down on her again, and the action made my headphones slip off my ears. They hung down on my chest and I hurriedly thrust them back onto my ears. That done, I quickly swung the chunk of concrete down again.

I'd been straddling the woman, but now I stood up and tossed the chunk of concrete onto her chest. The concrete bounced against her chest and clunked against the ground. The woman's face looked like it didn't have a chin any more. Black foam gurgled from her mouth. Just as I was about to leave, the woman's hand moved a fraction. I bent over and saw she was pushing her thumb, over and over, against the button on the umbrella.

At that very instant someone grabbed my wrist from behind. Wet from the rain, my wrist slipped away, but was grabbed again and roughly pulled. I recoiled and the headphones slipped off my ears again, slapping against my chest like a whip. They swung from side to side and hung down limply towards my feet. I lost my balance and may have stepped on the woman's stomach. My soles seemed to sink into something. I looked up and there stood Satoru, his face pale. He was holding an opened black umbrella, pointed down. I couldn't tell if it was me who was trembling, or Satoru as he held my wrist. The instant I saw him, and saw how tense he was, all the energy drained out of my body. It was a pleasant feeling, like my skin was being tickled.

I was about to say something to him, but shut my mouth. For some reason, I almost thanked him.

Right then Satoru's mouth moved. 'Hurry up!' he said and pulled my arm hard. I stepped on the woman's stomach again. Satoru pulled me even harder. 'Hurry up!' he repeated. We left the shadows of the pillar and went to the median. Satoru never let go of my arm. I didn't resist being pulled along, but was concerned about the headphones that had been tugged away from my ears and I tried to haul them in. They hung down like a tail as we trotted along, and I couldn't grab them.

I can't remember what I was thinking about as Satoru yanked me along towards Ryosuke's car park. Maybe I was only concerned about my headphones dragging along.

At the car park the gravel crunched under our feet as we ran towards Ryosuke's car. I was moving too slow for his liking and he shoved me hard into the passenger side seat, locking the door so I wouldn't escape, I suppose, then he ran round the front of the car and into the driver's side seat. He slammed the door shut. The sounds outside were shut out, and all I could hear was the rain pounding on the roof. Maybe because of this, all the tension that had built up drained away. 'Man, I'm soaked,' Satoru said. He twisted around and shoved the wet umbrella in the back seat. Something's about to begin now, I thought. But I couldn't help but think it would be something very pleasant. I know it was kind of arrogant of me, but when I looked at Satoru's soaked face, I nearly smiled. And at the same time I noticed how terribly self-conscious I was.

'It's okay. Nobody saw you, and we didn't see anybody else on the way over here,' Satoru said as he tugged off his wet T-shirt. I couldn't figure out what he was talking about. Satoru pulled a bath towel from the back seat, wiped his face and chest, wadded it up and thrust it towards me. I knew I was supposed to say something, but I couldn't find the words. It felt like if I didn't say something everything would be over.

Satoru yanked a dry T-shirt from a bag in the back seat. It was like he wasn't paying any attention to me at all. Feeling like I was getting used to being ignored, I hurriedly grabbed his shoulder.

'Hey!' I said. 'What do you think you're doing? You've got to turn me in to the police right away!' My throat was shaking, and felt sweetly painful.

'Jeez – You scared me half to death . . .' Satoru looked annoyed at my sudden outburst.

I waited for his next words, thinking that when he asked me *Why did you do it?* I'd finally have a chance to explain this to myself. But Satoru just held out the T-shirt he'd taken out and told me to put it on. I was just sitting there vacantly. He reached out to try to tug off my wet T-shirt. 'Knock it off!' I shouted, brushing aside his hand. But still he reached out to me.

'It's all right. You gotta hurry,' he said.

'What's changing my shirt going to do!' I yelled.

'There's blood all over the one you have on,' Satoru replied.

'So what?!'

'You can't go home looking like that!'

I see. So I'm going home. Satoru's going to take me back and reveal me for who I am, in front of everyone.

Satoru peeled the sopping T-shirt from my unresisting body. Urged on by him to 'Hurry up!' I put on the dry T-shirt. It had a milky smell to it, and was a little too small. I pictured how pitiful I'd look, handed over in front of everyone. But then I imagined myself yelling at them *You have no right to blame me!* and it made me feel kind of cheerful.

'Okay? Have you finished changing?'

The moment Satoru opened the driver's side door, the car was swallowed up in the sound from outside. The sound of the rain beating against the gravel. Far-off lightning flashed in the sky. He handed me a plastic bag and I shoved the wet T-shirt inside. I shoved it in so hard the rain and sweat and blood seeped out and soaked my hand.

Satoru, open umbrella in hand, walked around to the passenger side. He pressed his face up against the glass and watched as I tied up the plastic bag. When I opened the door, Satoru, who'd taken a step back, held the umbrella over me as I got out of the car.

'I wonder if everybody's back by now.'

Satoru's voice, mixed in with the crunch of gravel, sounded a little too carefree. Without replying, I snatched the umbrella from him.

I walked along next to him for a while. I don't know why, but it felt crushingly boring. What I wanted was to be quickly exposed for who I am. A couple of times while we were walking Satoru told me, 'It'll be okay.' Each time he did I repeated to myself, *There's no way it's going to be okay. You didn't see that woman's face*. I knew he glanced at me a few times, but I deliberately avoided his eyes. The image of the woman's face, smashed by the chunk of concrete, came and went in my mind's eye. The woman might still be there, undiscovered, leaning against the fence under the elevated bridge, her thumb still pushing the button on her umbrella.

We cut through an alley in a residential neighbourhood, took a different street and came out on Route 20. Cars buzzed past, shooting up spray from the wet asphalt. The long white lines of the crossing looked like a bridge over a dark river. Satoru gave my back a push and I stepped forwards. The crossing signal had turned green before I realised it. The headlights of the line of cars stopped at the stop line shone on Satoru and me. We were lit up, but that light only grazed our skin, wet from the rain, and didn't shine inside us.

'What do you plan to tell them?' I asked, as I was just nearing the other side.

'Well . . . I'm not going to say anything.'

I came to an abrupt halt. Did I hear him wrong? Satoru, still walking, took a step forwards out from under the umbrella. He turned around, his face contorted in the rain, and was looking at me.

'Hurry up!'

He grabbed my wrist again, but I shook free. Rattled, I asked, 'What do you mean you're not going to say anything?'

Satoru was gazing steadily at me. 'Doesn't everybody already know?' he murmured, sounding annoyed.

'They already know?'

I grabbed him by the shoulders. His shoulders were so thin. 'It hurts,' he said, twisting away.

'Who do you mean, *everybody*?'

'Everybody means everybody. Mirai, Ryosuke, and Koto. Don't they all know? I'm not really sure, though, since I never talked with them about it.'

He sounded totally peeved. 'Hurry up!' he said again and pulled me by the arm.

'Hold on. If everybody knows, then why didn't they say anything?'

'How should *I* know?'

'Why didn't *you* say anything?'

'I don't know. Nobody said anything . . . And besides, I like living there.'

I suddenly recalled Ryosuke and Koto's faces when I was going out jogging and they were just coming back from the video store. They saw my jogging shoes and looked a little put out. Satoru's voice came back to me, his insistence that everything would be

I gazed at the girl's face as she ran her tongue over the guy's cock. I remembered Mirai getting splashed with water at Halcyon, but I didn't remember the face of the girl who did it. Mirai, arms folded, glared at me. 'You remember her?' she said, but I just stood there, dumbfounded, and shook my head.

From the bathroom behind me I heard Satoru's voice. 'Did you just get in?' 'No, I'll be out in a minute,' Ryosuke shouted back from inside the bath. Satoru emerged from the changing area next to the bath and, for some reason I couldn't fathom, shot me a huge grin as I stood there at the entrance to the living room. Satoru pushed past me and plopped down next to Koto. Koto looked up from the mirror and turned to him.

'Look okay?' she asked.

'The right one looks a little thick,' Satoru replied, and Koto peered back in the mirror.

Mirai, towering over them, asked, 'You think this girl's pretty?' poking Satoru in the back with her foot.

Satoru looked up at the TV. 'No, I don't. Is she some friend of yours?'

'She's the one who threw water on me.'

'How come?'

'I have no idea. She was showing off a huge diamond ring – an engagement ring, maybe, I don't know – and I said *Do you have any idea how many African children were sacrificed to make this diamond?* and she said I was just jealous. It pissed me off and I threw some peanuts in her face. And she flung a glass of water at me.'

'Didn't you fling one back?'

'Of course I was about to. But then Saint Naoki here pinned me down and kept me from doing it.'

In tandem Mirai and Satoru turned around to look at me. Right then Ryosuke, bath towel wrapped around his waist, emerged from the bathroom. 'Excuse me,' he said his wet back bumping my arm as he squeezed past. 'The bath's all yours,' he said to Satoru. 'But I wanted to take a bath,' Koto said, poking Satoru. Nobody seemed to care about me. And that's when it hit me. I could feel it in my bones that they really knew. That they really had known.

'So what are you going to do about school?' Ryosuke, seated on the sofa now, asked Satoru, tapping him on the head. Next to them Koto gave a big yawn, while Mirai, standing there with remote in hand, was glaring at the TV. As with all the times before, all I had to do was take a step forwards, and things might be all right.

The first night I attacked a woman on the streets, Koto, wearing a face pack, asked me, 'What kind of guy is this Umezaki? Ryosuke asked me to go to Izu Kogen with him.' Pretending to be as calm as I could, I just replied, 'He's a good guy.' The second time, when I came home, Ryosuke and Mirai, both looking pretty serious, asked me, 'This guy sleeping on the sofa this morning – did you bring him here?' I should have just said, 'I have no idea.' The third time, after attacking the woman I helped take care of Mirai, who'd come home dead drunk. The fourth time, I didn't sleep a wink the whole night, and that's when I asked Satoru, who was eating waffles that morning, if he'd like to work part-time at my office.

Like all the times before, as long as I took a step forwards, then everything might be settled.

I was still standing at the entrance to the living room. The woman's face suddenly came to me, the one I'd crushed with a chunk of concrete. She might still be lying there in the rain, under the dark, elevated bridge. If, say, there were another Tokyo in this world, and that woman were lying there, I'm sure I would rush off to rescue her.

Laughing voices echoed in front of me. Before I knew it, the TV was showing pink panthers dancing around. This had to be that video of Mirai's. The pink panthers that had been recorded over those ghastly rape scenes . . . A parade of smiling pink panthers, shaking their hips as they danced.

Ryosuke was on the sofa, Koto and Satoru, the good friends, sat side by side, and Mirai was still planted in front of the TV – all of them were laughing, ignoring me. I was left hanging, by the doorway, unjudged, unforgiven, null and void. It was as if they had already – in place of me – felt regret, repented, and asked for forgiveness. We're not going to give you anything, they seemed to be telling me. You can forget about the right to explain yourself, confess, or apologise – we'll never give it to you. It felt like they hated me, their disgust implacable and unrelenting.